About Apollo Africa

The original Heinemann African Writers Series was launched in 1962 with the publication of Chinua Achebe's *Things Fall Apart*, Cyprian Ekwensi's *Burning Grass* and Kenneth Kaunda's *Zambia Shall Be Free*, with Achebe himself acting as an editorial advisor. Over the next 40 years, the series continued to publish the best writing from across the African continent.

One of the founding aims of the Heinemann series was to make books by African writers available to as wide a readership as possible. Apollo Africa – a collaboration between Black Star Books and Head of Zeus – is proud to continue this work, ensuring novels, essays, poetry and plays from the original series are once again made available to readers all over the world.

Behind the Clouds

Behind the Clouds

Ifeoma Okoye

Black Star Books and Head of Zeus would like to thank the following organisations: The Miles Morland Foundation, The Ford Foundation, and Africa No Filter. This publication was made possible through their support.

First published in the Longman African Writers Series in 1982 by Pearson Education Limited

This edition published in 2023 by Black Star Books and Head of Zeus, part of Bloomsbury Publishing Plc.

Copyright © Ifeoma Okoye, 1982

The moral right of Ifeoma Okoye to be identified as the author of this work has been asserted in accordance with the Copyright, Designs and Patents Act of 1988.

All rights reserved. No part of this publication may be reproduced, stored in a retrieval system, or transmitted in any form or by any means, electronic, mechanical, photocopying, recording, or otherwise, without the prior permission of both the copyright owner and the above publisher of this book.

This reprint is published by arrangement with Pearson Education Limited.

This is a work of fiction. All characters, organizations, and events portrayed in this novel are either products of the author's imagination or are used fictitiously.

9 7 5 3 1 2 4 6 8

A catalogue record for this book is available from the British Library.

ISBN (PB): 9781035900732
ISBN (E): 9781803288437

Typeset by Siliconchips Services Ltd UK

Printed and bound in Great Britain by
CPI Group (UK) Ltd, Croydon CR0 4YY

Head of Zeus Ltd
First Floor East
5–8 Hardwick Street
London EC1R 4RG

WWW.HEADOFZEUS.COM

Be still, sad heart! and cease repining;
Behind the clouds is the sun still shining.

The Rainy Day,
HENRY WADSWORTH LONGFELLOW

To my peerless and impeccable 'Osiris', with love

Chapter One

Ije Apia arrived at the Blest Clinic at about half-past seven in the morning. A middle-aged cleaner who was dusting the panes of a window showed her the clinic's waiting-room. Ije walked in quietly. A handful of patients were already in the room. Some of them were standing round the clinic's clerk, waiting to be registered. Ije joined them and waited for her turn. When it came, she paid her registration fee to the clerk, obtained a receipt, a hospital card, and a numbered card. In spite of her early arrival she would be the seventeenth patient to see the doctor.

'That will mean a long wait,' Ije said under her breath as she put the registration card, the receipt and the numbered card into her handbag.

She walked past patients who were sitting dejectedly on a couple of long settees until she came to two empty armchairs at the end of the room. Here was what she wanted: a quiet place where she could sit undisturbed by other patients. With her handkerchief she dusted one of the armchairs and sat down in it to wait for her turn to see the doctor.

The waiting-room of the clinic was neat and clean – quite unlike the waiting-rooms of the other private clinics she had visited. The pale blue walls of the room were adorned with beautiful pictures and posters. There was a poster showing the different stages of foetal growth. There was another one on vitamins and the foodstuffs that contain them. A third poster was on child-care. Ije looked around her with silent approval.

Seconds later she was lost in thought, oblivious of the bustle in the waiting-room as more patients arrived and nurses strutted in and out. It was becoming increasingly difficult for her, especially when she was alone, to keep her mind off her predicament.

As Ije sat there, her mind plunged deep into the past: a past full of failures that still rankled. She remembered vividly all the doctors who had treated her – the tests, the minor operations, and the major one that had almost killed her. She remembered also the herbalists she had approached for help.

The first herbalist she had consulted had said she was an *ogbanje* from the river and her *ogbanje* mates were responsible for her problem.

'Why are they against me?' Ije had asked the herbalist.

'Because you violated your joint vow not to marry,' the herbalist had told her.

'Can't anything be done about it?' Ije had inquired.

'Yes, we can appease them with a sacrifice,' was the herbalist's reply.

Ije's religious code could not at first be reconciled with the herbalist's suggestion but her strong desire to overcome her problem had outweighed both her loyalty to her religion and her reason. With reluctance she had consented to offer the sacrifice. Months later, it became clear to her that the oblation was in vain and so also were the herbalist's concoctions that she was made to drink.

Then there was the other herbalist who had attributed her problem to the evil machinations of her enemies. The herbalist had boasted that he knew the names of these enemies but had refused to disclose them. Instead, he had claimed to possess the powers to counteract their evil plans, and had extorted a large sum of money from her to 'buy what he needed for his battle with the powers of evil'. Again nothing had come of this.

There was one herbalist who, Ije believed, could have done something for her, but she was too late. On her arrival at the man's house, she was told that the man had died a week earlier. The herbalist, unfortunately, did not pass on his knowledge of herbs and roots to any of his sons because, according to him, none was pious or level-headed enough to be trusted with such knowledge.

Ije had been crestfallen to hear of the man's death. 'Why had I not known about this man earlier?' she kept saying to herself throughout her journey home. It was at this time, when she was at the nadir of her hopes, that she learned of the 'miracles' wrought by one Dr Melie who had opened a clinic in town: 'The Blest Clinic'. At first she was sceptical about seeing another doctor as her optimism had been eroded by her fruitless visits to so many doctors.

'Paper!' a newsvendor called, breaking into Ije's thoughts and bringing her back to the present. 'Madam, you want paper?' The vendor was now standing in front of her.

'Yes, give me a copy of *New Nigerian*,' Ije said. 'And a copy of *Daily Times*.'

'I have some beautiful magazines, too,' the newsvendor tried to coax her.

'I don't want anything more,' Ije said and paid him for the newspapers.

As the vendor walked away, Ije began to scan the newspapers while she waited for her turn to see the doctor. Presently, she was interrupted by a fat woman who came and sat down in the armchair next to hers.

'Good morning,' the woman greeted her.

'Good morning,' Ije replied, lifting up her eyes and resting them on the woman. She had a short neck. Her small head rested on her shoulders and her large bosom rose and fell as she breathed heavily. She was extravagantly made up and was dressed in a flowered *buba* and *lappa*.

'Is your name Ije?' the fat woman asked.

'Yes,' Ije replied. There was a blank look on her face as she gazed at the woman whom she did not recognise.

The fat woman noticed Ije's bewilderment. 'I won't blame you for not recognising me,' she said, smiling. 'I've grown very fat – fat beyond recognition. But can't you guess?'

Ije's eyes narrowed as she looked at the woman. She tried again to recollect where she had seen her before but drew a blank. She gave up.

'Honestly. I can't remember who you are,' she said apologetically. 'My memory is like a sieve these days.'

'You were once at A.C.M. Port Harcourt, weren't you?' the fat woman inquired.

'Yes.'

'And you were in Warner House?'

'You're right,' Ije admitted.

'Remember Beatrice? The sprinter? I was in class three when you were in four, I think.'

Ije's face lit up with recognition. 'Yes, I remember you now,' she said. 'But you were slimmer then.'

'Yes, I was,' Beatrice agreed. 'I wish I had not grown so fat. My husband nags me day and night because of my obesity. That's the word he uses to describe my condition. You live here in Enugu?'

'Yes,' Ije replied. 'And you?'

'My husband and I have just come to Enugu on transfer. We lived in Abakaliki until a few months ago.'

'I see,' Ije said, folding her newspapers and putting them away in her handbag.

'Have you been here before?' Beatrice asked.

'You mean to this hospital?'

'Yes.'

'No. This is my first time,' Ije explained.

'This is my first time, too. I understand this Dr Melie is very good.'

'So I was told.'

'Are you having trouble, too?' Beatrice asked.

'Yes,' Ije replied. She wished she could stop the conversation. She was not used to discussing her personal problems with outsiders.

But Beatrice was one of those women who confide easily in people. She told Ije about her problems. She had been married for eight years without a child. She had been to many gynaecologists and to several herbalists but none had been able to help her.

'My husband is very worried,' Beatrice continued, mopping her face with a handkerchief. She was now sweating profusely even though it was not hot. Her large bosom rose and fell as she breathed heavily.

'My husband is worried to death,' Beatrice reiterated. 'His parents, his relations, his friends, all keep on telling him to get himself another wife to bear him an heir. I'm sure that one of these days he'll heed their advice. He's getting fed up with me. He flares up at me most of the time no matter what I do.'

She stopped talking because she was out of breath.

Ije said nothing. She did not want to discuss her own problems with Beatrice, so she thought it unfair to encourage her to continue discussing hers.

But Beatrice rattled on, taking no notice of Ije's silence. She told Ije about the many quarrels she had had with her husband because of her childlessness. She talked about her mother-in-law pouring abuse on her.

In answer to her question Ije told her that she, too, had no child although she had been married for years.

Beatrice was genuinely sorry for Ije in spite of her own misfortune.

'I don't know why in this country of ours it is always the women who take all the blame when a couple is childless,' she said contemptuously. She became silent for a while.

Just then a pregnant woman walked into the waiting-room. Beatrice went over to her and they talked for a few minutes. Then she came back and resumed her seat beside Ije.

'Did you see that woman I talked to just now?' Beatrice asked excitedly.

'The pregnant one?'

'Yes, that one,' Beatrice said. 'She has been married for a good fifteen years without a child. And now God has blessed her for her patience!'

'She's lucky,' Ije rejoined.

'Very lucky indeed. And her husband is a gentleman. He has doted on her for these fifteen years in spite of pressures from his parents and relations to take a second wife. The woman is from my village. She's a very good woman.'

'And God has rewarded her for her virtue,' Ije thought aloud.

'Not all virtuous people are lucky,' Beatrice rejoined. She stood up. 'I'll be back in a minute,' she said and wobbled out of the waiting-room.

Ije was again left to her own thoughts. She wondered if her husband would be patient enough to wait for fifteen years for a child from her. Her mind went back to London. She remembered the first day she met her husband, Dozie. It was at a friend's wedding. The bridegroom was Dozie's classmate, so he had come to the wedding. She remembered their happy courtship. Dozie was quite different from most of the Nigerian men in London in those days. He was shy, faithful, and kind.

Ije's room-mate in the hostel had disapproved of Dozie. She had told Ije bluntly that Dozie had nothing to offer her; that Dozie was after her because she was working and could give him financial support. Ije now remembered vividly her roommate's last words on the issue.

'You're behaving like an Englishwoman, Ije,' she had said. 'Remember you're dealing with a Nigerian. In Nigeria, men maintain women and not the other way round. Dozie will not respect you for it.'

But Dozie's behaviour since they were married had given the lie to her friend's opinions. Now, after more than five years of being married to him, Ije had nothing to complain about. Their life had been one of give and take; a life full of the joys of sharing. They had learnt to understand each other; to be able to communicate even without speaking. They had grown to be as much as possible one flesh, and whatever social life they had, they had together.

'If only God would bless us with a child,' Ije whispered to herself.

At this moment Beatrice returned, interrupting Ije's train of thought.

'Well,' she said, breathing heavily, 'if Dr Melie fails me I'll turn to the faith-healers. Didn't Jesus say prayers can move mountains?'

Ije wanted to correct her. The Bible says faith, not prayers. But she changed her mind. She did not think much of the so-called faith-healers anyway, but she kept her own counsel.

It was now her turn to go in and see the doctor.

'We'll meet again,' she said to Beatrice, and walked into the doctor's consulting-room.

Dr Melie, a handsome man in his early forties, was busy scribbling on a pad when Ije entered his consulting room. Absentmindedly, he replied to Ije's greeting and motioned her to a chair opposite him. Ije sat down and waited patiently for him to finish whatever he was writing.

'Yes, young lady, what is your problem?' Dr Melie inquired, putting away his scribbling-block. While he waited for an answer to his question he glanced at Ije's card, taking a mental note of her age, occupation and other such particulars.

Tears welled into Ije's eyes and she pressed her fingers against them. In spite of her resolution to be stoical about her misfortune, she could not help being wet-eyed whenever she wanted to talk about it.

The tears refused to be kept in and she dabbed her eyes again and again with her handkerchief. Presently she said with tears in her voice:

'I want a baby, doctor.'

Dr Melie looked at her sympathetically. He saw a well-built woman, dark, with a good crop of jet-black hair which she had combed back and held with a hair-ring. She was slim, and her dark skin was as smooth and as translucent as a new-born baby's. Dr Melie noticed that she wore no make-up – hers was a natural unadulterated prettiness.

'How long have you been married, young lady?' Dr Melie asked.

'Nearly six years, doctor.'

Dr Melie looked at her card again. 'You're only thirty-three, young lady,' he said, studying her face. 'There's still plenty of time for you to have all the babies you want. Now cheer up. You're not at the end of the road yet.'

'For a year after I married, doctor, I did not want a baby, but since I decided to start a family I – I – I –' She stopped speaking because the lump in her throat was choking her.

'It's all right, young lady, I understand,' Dr Melie said kindly. 'Now tell me, why did you not want to start a family immediately you were married?'

'My husband had not finished his course at the university. He was having some difficulty paying his fees and could not combine his studies with going to work. I had to keep two jobs in order to help him pay his university fees. That was in London. My jobs were difficult ones. My husband and I therefore decided it would be too much for me to hold down the jobs if I became pregnant. We had to defer starting a family until later.'

'Were you on the pill then?'

'No, doctor. I was scared stiff of such things.'

'Any "accidents"?' Dr Melie asked.

Ije understood the euphemism which the doctor had used for unplanned pregnancies.

'There was none, doctor,' she said.

She remembered now how much she had dreaded any 'accidents' during those days in London and how happy she had felt at the end of every month when it was clear to her that she was free. These days it was the other way round. She approached the end of each month with apprehension and became miserable as she watched her dreams dissolve into nothingness as the months came and went.

'Do you live with your husband now?' Dr Melie broke into Ije's thoughts.

'Yes, doctor.'

'And you have always lived together?'

'Yes, doctor.'

'What is his job?'

Ije wondered what this had to do with her problem. Then she remembered having read somewhere that some jobs lower fertility, especially in men.

'My husband is an architect,' she said.

'Had any kidney trouble?'

'No, doctor.'

'Tuberculosis?'

Ije shook her head.

'Any miscarriages?'

'None. I've never conceived, doctor.'

Dr Melie wrote continually, lifting his head once in a while to look at his patient.

'Any surgical operations?' Dr Melie asked, lifting up his head to look at Ije.

'Yes. Many of them,' Ije said and listed them. She had had her appendix out; had had many D & Cs; had also had an operation for fibroids.

'You said you had an operation for fibroids?'

'Yes, doctor,' Ije reaffirmed. 'That was two years ago.'

She suppressed the urge to add that she had learnt from a reliable source after the operation that she had not really had fibroids; that the doctor's diagnosis had been wrong; and that he had realised his mistake only after he had opened her up in the theatre. She shuddered as she remembered all that she had gone through at that time. She had lost a lot of blood and would have bled to death if she had not had a blood transfusion. As if that was not enough, her suture had grown septic and had taken weeks to heal.

Then Ije said aloud: 'I've been to several doctors. I've

had many kinds of tests. I've had different kinds of treatments, but all of them have been in vain. You're my last hope, doctor. My friends tell me you're very good. Please, do your best for me.'

'I'll do what I can for you, young lady,' Dr Melie said. He always addressed women as 'young lady' even when strands of grey hair that had mischievously escaped the hair dye betrayed the truth.

Dr Melie motioned Ije to the door of his examination room. 'Go in there and undress, Mrs Apia,' he said. 'I'd like to examine you.'

Ije rose and walked to the door. A nurse followed her into the room and closed the door behind her. A few minutes later, Ije was back on her chair in the consulting room. The examination was over. The pain caused her by Dr Melie's palpations still lingered in her as she waited for him to finish scrubbing his hands.

Later, Dr Melie sat down in his chair and asked the nurse to give him a new booklet of prescription forms.

'Well, Mrs Apia,' he said when he had finished writing on the form, 'I've prescribed some medicines for you which you will collect at the dispensary. I'd like you to have some tests and X-rays too. I've filled out the forms for these. Come and see me again next week. I hope the results of the tests will be ready by then.' He told Ije his charge, and looked steadily at her to see her reaction.

Ije's face was expressionless. She was used to paying

huge amounts of money to doctors. In her predicament she had always felt that no amount of money was too much to pay for a baby. Besides, money was no problem to her. Her husband was doing well in his business. He, too, was desperately in need of a child and was ready to pay anything for it.

Ije opened her handbag, brought out a brown envelope, and from it she counted out ten new twenty-naira notes while Dr Melie looked at her through the corner of his eyes. Ije handed over the money to him and watched him count the notes, wondering why he did not employ an accounts clerk to collect his money for him.

'Well, Mrs Apia,' Dr Melie said, putting the money into a drawer in his table and locking the drawer securely, 'As I said, I'll see you again in a week's time. You don't have to queue up with the other patients when you arrive. Come right in and I'll see you at once.'

Ije thanked him and walked out of the room wondering why all the doctors she had consulted so far had given her preferential treatment. Was it because her case was a special one or was it because she could afford to pay any amount of money demanded of her without pleading for a reduction?

Outside the building, Ije looked at her watch. It was a little past twelve noon. She decided to do some shopping before going home. Since she resigned her job as an accountant in an insurance company, she had been doing most of the family's shopping although she had a reliable steward who would do it for her without cheating her. She also had a maid, not very clever, but faithful.

As Ije drove out of the clinic, her hopes rose and she prayed silently to God to grant her her wish.

Chapter Two

There was not much traffic as Ije drove through Kenyatta Street into Edozie Street. But it took her minutes to join Zik Avenue from Edozie Street. The traffic here was heavy. It usually was at that time of the day. The vehicles crawled along the avenue like giant tortoises, while the taxi drivers, incorrigible as ever, wove through the traffic as if only they had reason to be in a hurry.

When Ije came to Leventis Stores, she decided to stop and buy a few food items. She parked her car where it would be easy for her to join the ever-busy Zik Avenue again. She was about to enter the shop when someone called out greetings from a car parked nearby. Ije retraced her steps and a man got out of the car and walked towards her.

'Hello, Ije,' the man said. 'How are you?'

'Fine, and you?' Ije said.

'So-so,' the man answered. He was a very senior official in one of the Government Ministries. He had been in London when Ije was there and had proposed to her. She had turned him down, although he had better prospects then than Dozie whom she later married.

'How are your family?' Ije asked.

'Fine,' the man answered. He was married to a podgy woman and they had five children: two girls and three boys. Ije knew the wife and had seen the children once, pretty, sweet children who were in no way like their mother.

As Ije looked at the man she wondered if he would have been so blessed with children if he had married her instead of his podgy wife.

'You're scarce these days, Ije,' the man said. 'I still can't understand why you refused me.'

'Oh, don't let's go into that again,' Ije cut in. 'I must be going. I want to buy a few things from the shop.'

'I must say you're looking very trim, Ije,' the man said, reluctant to let her go. 'You've kept your figure. That's what I like to see in women.'

Ije saw his last statement as a criticism of his wife. She was right, as the man's next sentence proved.

'I wish you'd tell my wife your secret,' he said.

Ije chuckled and said lightly: 'It's because I don't have enough food to eat.' She wanted to say that it was because she had never had children, but she had changed her mind. It was not proper for her to wear her misfortune on her forehead for everyone to see.

'Nonsense,' the man said with a smile. 'Not enough to eat indeed! I'd say rather it's because you eat sensibly.'

'Bye,' Ije said and went into the shop.

She looked around the shop for a while, bought a few things and left. The traffic on Zik Avenue was still heavy. She got into her car, and after what seemed an eternity she managed to squeeze into the seemingly endless line of vehicles on the avenue.

She stopped briefly at Kingsway Stores in Okpara Avenue, paid for two crates of drinks that a friend had reserved for her, and drove home.

James, her steward, saw her arrive home and ran to open the front door for her.

'Welcome, madam,' he said as he helped her bring out the things from her car. He was about twenty-three, and small for his age. His high intelligence, however, made up for what he lacked in stature.

'Have you prepared the ingredients for soup, James?'

'Yes, madam.' He was walking ahead of her, laden with two polythene bags.

'Put those things away in the kitchen store, James,' Ije said as they came into the sitting-room. 'I'll come to cook the soup in a few minutes' time.'

'Yes, madam.'

Ije sat down in one of the deep armchairs in the sitting-room and kicked off her shoes. Then she remembered that she had left the front door open. She got up and walked barefoot to the door. She closed it and turned the key in the lock. The year before, she had left the front door open and a clever rogue had walked into the sitting-room and carried off a transistor radio. The theft was not discovered until later in the evening when her husband had wanted to listen to the six o'clock news.

As Ije sat down again she was overcome by a sudden

depression. Her mind went back to the hospital. Dr Melie's words rang in her ears. 'I'll do what I can for you,' he had said. She wondered whether he would succeed where others had failed. She was now turning into a pessimist, not by design, but because each ray of hope had been dashed by the events that followed it.

Ije's maid, Teresa, came in at this moment, waking her from the stupor of grief into which she had fallen. She lifted her sad eyes and rested them on Teresa.

'Where have you been, Teresa?'

'In the boys' quarters washing clothes,' Teresa replied. She was about nineteen, fair-complexioned and plump. Her small pretty face was made prettier by her small eyes that seemed always to be smiling.

'Go and help James in the kitchen.'

'Yes, madam,' Teresa said, and left the room.

A few minutes later, Ije went into the kitchen to cook the soup for lunch.

'Madam, I forgot to tell you say Master telephoned,' James said. His mother-tongue was different from Ije's because they came from different parts of the country so he always spoke to her in his poor English.

'What did Master say?' Ije inquired, turning the soup on the fire with a silver-plated spoon.

'He say you get ready to go for party in the night. He say he will be late for afternoon food.'

Ije began to remove the bones from the dried fish she would put in the soup.

'Now bring the vegetables, James,' she said when she had finished with the fish.

James handed over to her a plate of vegetables which he had shredded and washed. Ije put the vegetables into the soup-pot on the fire, turned the soup with a spoon, and then put in the pieces of dried fish.

Ije stirred the soup again, put on the lid, then went to the kitchen sink and washed her hands.

'Watch the soup, James,' she said, drying her hands with a small towel. 'Don't let it get burnt. It will boil for another twenty minutes or so before it is done. And you, Teresa, wash up and boil some water for garri.'

Satisfied with her division of labour, Ije went back to the sitting-room.

Dozie returned after three o'clock in the afternoon. Ije was still in the sitting-room waiting for him to come home so that they could have lunch together.

'Did James tell you I telephoned?' Dozie sat down and began to unlace his shoes.

'Yes, he did,' Ije replied. 'You're late for lunch today, D.'

'I'm sorry. Someone came from Nsukka to see me. I didn't finish with him in time. Did you see the doctor?'

Ije rose. 'Yes, I did,' she said. 'Let me tell James to bring lunch first.' She took her husband's briefcase into the bedroom and then went into the kitchen. A few minutes later she and Dozie sat down to lunch.

'What did Dr Melie say?' Dozie asked as he took a large helping of garri.

Ije became sullen. She stopped eating for a second. 'He says he can't tell what is wrong with me until I've had some tests.'

'Did he tell you what kind of tests?'

'Yes.'

'What are they?'

'X-rays, blood tests, urine tests, and one other one. I've forgotten what he called it. They always send me for tests and nothing happens afterwards.'

'What do you do after the tests?'

'Go to see him, of course.'

'Cheer up, Ije. Don't look so sad,' Dozie tried to console her. 'We'll have our children some day. It's hard on you. I know that. It's hard on me, too.'

Ije shrank into deep silence. Her mind went back to their days in London. She remembered vividly the day Dozie had graduated. They had invited a handful of friends to celebrate the occasion with them. When their friends had gone, and they were alone, Dozie had told her how anxious he was to have his children since there was nothing more holding them back. His words came back to her. 'Ije,' he had said, 'I want a girl from you first. A girl who would be a carbon-copy of you.' That was about five years ago.

'Sh – sh,' Dozie shooed to bring Ije back from her bemused state. 'What are you thinking about?'

'How I have failed you,' Ije said. There were tears in her voice.

'Nonsense!' Dozie said. 'Who said you have failed me?'

'I know I have.'

'You have not failed me, Ije,' Dozie said tenderly. 'I have not lost hope of your ever bearing my children. We are not the only ones who are or who have been in this position. If others have succeeded in the end, why can't we?'

Dozie loved children and Ije knew he did. That was one of the reasons why she felt their misfortune very much. He had been a good husband to her: kind, generous, and loving. To her, his only fault so far was his inability to make decisions easily. He would keep postponing taking a stand on issues and would reconsider several times the decisions when he had taken them. When he had found himself in such a predicament, as he often did, he would let her wisdom produce a suggestion and she had always come to his rescue. She would subtly tell him what to do without sounding bossy or making him look a fool.

They finished their meal in silence. Then they went back to the sitting-room. Dozie asked for a toothpick and began to pick his teeth.

'Sorry I didn't tell you about the party in time,' he said. 'I left the invitation card in my office and forgot all about it until I saw it again this morning.'

'Whose party is it?' Ije asked.

'Mr Ude's. One of his expatriate engineers is leaving Nigeria for good and he's giving a send-off party in his honour.'

'What type of party?'

'Buffet.'

'I see,' Ije said.

Teresa came into the dining-room and began to clear the table. Ije could see her head and shoulders above the dwarf wall that separated the dining-room from the sitting-room. 'Teresa!' she called.

'Yes, madam?'

'Tell James we'll have no supper to-night. You two can cook whatever you like for your own supper.'

'Yes, madam.' She gathered the plates and went into the kitchen.

'The party is at eight,' Dozie said, 'but we can leave at seven and spend about an hour in the Sports Club. You look depressed and a change of atmosphere will do you some good. I don't want you to go to the party looking as if you're carrying the burden of the whole world on your fragile shoulders.'

Ije remained silent.

'Can you be ready by that time?' Dozie asked.

'Of course I can. I don't spend hours trying to decide what to wear.'

'Is that what makes some women waste so much time in getting ready for parties or church services?'

'That's one of the reasons,' Ije said. A little smile flickered over her face.

Five minutes later Dozie had nodded off in his chair, snoring faintly.

Ije thought: he must have overworked himself in the office. She rose from her chair and went to him.

'D., D.,' she called faintly, tapping him gently on the shoulder.

'M – m – m,' Dozie mumbled. He tried to look at Ije through heavy eyelids.

'Get up and go to bed,' she said to him.

Dozie opened his eyes and stifled a yawn. 'I didn't realise I had dropped off,' he said, rising from his chair. 'You, too, need a rest after spending hours in the hospital, don't you?'

He walked into the bedroom and a little later Ije joined him.

The evening was cool after the intense heat of the afternoon. Dozie slept till six o'clock. Ije, who had lain beside him without sleeping, sat up in bed and shook him gently to wake him up.

'I think you've slept enough, D.,' she said, 'or else you'll find it difficult to sleep in the night.'

Dozie stretched himself, rubbed his eyes with his hands and sat up on the bed beside Ije.

'Did you sleep?' he asked.

'No, I couldn't.'

'Why not?'

'I don't know,' Ije said. 'My mind kept wandering.'

Dozie put his arm round her shoulders. 'I've told you not to worry yourself too much, Ije,' he admonished her gently.

Ije said nothing. A brooding silence fell between them.

She knew that Dozie sometimes worried about their plight too, but being the man he was he always tried to hide his anxiety if only to make her take their misfortune lightly.

'I'll run your bath for you,' Ije said and stood up.

'No. I'm not ready to wash now,' Dozie said. 'You go and wash. I want to look for an important document which I need in the office tomorrow.'

'Do you want me to help you look for it?' Ije asked.

'No. Don't worry. I'll find it. It must be in either of two places.'

Ije went into the bathroom and Dozie went to the bedroom he had turned into an office and began rummaging in a desk drawer for the document he wanted.

By seven o'clock Dozie and Ije were ready for the party. Dozie was dressed in a grey suit which fitted him superbly. He was a tall, handsome man. He was nearer fair-skinned than dark-skinned – a sort of pleasing balance between the two. He had allowed his hair to grow into two thin lines down the sides of his face.

Ije was dressed in a dark-red maxi dress which blended with her ebony-black skin. She too was tall but on the slim side. She was one of those women who can be described as neither beautiful nor ugly. Her beauty lay in her shapeliness, her sweet little mouth, and her simplicity. Her power to give pleasure was unsurpassed.

In the sitting-room Dozie rang the bell and in a few seconds James appeared.

'Sir?' he said reverently.

'We're going out and we'll be back late,' Dozie said to him. 'Lock the door when we have gone. We'll try and come back as soon as we can.'

'Yes, sir.'

'Where is Teresa?' Ije asked James.

'In her room.'

'What are you cooking for your supper?'

'Nothing, madam. We'll manage with the garri left.'

'From lunch?'

'Yes, madam.'

'You don't need to worry about them,' Dozie cut in. 'They're old enough to look after themselves. If they don't want any supper, that's their business. Let's go.'

They walked out of the house and James locked the front door after them.

There were not many people in the Sports Club when Dozie and Ije arrived. Those who had been playing tennis had gone home for a shower, so too had those who had come for a swim.

Dozie sighted an empty table in a corner of the main hall. He took Ije to the table and they sat down. Presently a man and his wife came to join them.

'Hello, Dozie,' the man greeted, extending his hand. Dozie stood up and shook it warmly.

'And how are you, Ije?' the man said. His wife stood aloof, watching.

'Fine,' Ije said, trying hard to be pleasant. She did not like the man. Once he had chaffed Dozie for always bringing his wife to the club. 'I've never seen you here alone,' he said to Dozie. 'Don't you want to be on your own sometimes?'

'I like her company,' Dozie had replied, laughing.

Now Ije waited for him to say something of the sort to Dozie again. Instead he told Dozie he would like to see him later to discuss something with him, and left. His wife walked timidly behind him.

'So it's true your friend has taken another wife,' Ije said to Dozie when the man and his wife were out of hearing. The man was a senior official in the Civil Service. A few weeks before, it had been rumoured that he had married again and that his former wife, who was British, had gone back to England in disgust. The man, it had been given out, had told his friends that he had married again because he could not take the 'Ozo title' with a white woman. Ije had not been taken in by this for she knew at least two Nigerians who had taken the title with their British wives.

'Of course I knew he had taken another wife,' Dozie said. 'I've seen him with that girl before.'

'Poor woman,' Ije thought aloud. 'Imagine leaving all her children to go home to England alone.' For one split second she imagined Dozie taking another wife. She thrust the offending and disloyal thought out of her mind, for it had scorched her like a live firebrand.

Dozie ordered some *suya*. He was about to order a bottle of beer for himself when Ije stopped him, reminding him that they were going to a party.

The waiter brought the *suya*. By the time they had finished eating it, it was time for them to leave for the party.

Chapter Three

Early the next day, Ije left for the clinic to have the tests and X-rays ordered by her doctor. She had no problem with the tests, but when she arrived at the X-ray department, she was told to wait because the electricity supply to the clinic had been cut off. Three hours later, the clinic was still without electric power and Ije was told to go home and come again the next day.

'How can I be sure you'll have electricity tomorrow?' Ije fumed.

'I can't tell, madam. Nobody is sure of NEPA these days,' the assistant radiographer said.

Still fuming at having spent so many hours in vain, Ije drove home.

'Welcome, madam,' James said politely as he opened the front door for her.

Ije replied to the greeting and went into the sitting-room. She sat down heavily, kicked off her shoes, removed her head-tie and placed it on a chair beside her.

'James, get me some water to drink, please,' she said. She was hot and tired, and her anger still lingered. She got up and switched on the ceiling fan.

Soon James was back with a bottle of ice-cold water and a glass. Ije drank two glasses of water without stopping. She filled the glass a third time and put it on a stool beside her.

'Did Master come home for lunch?' she asked James. When Dozie had too much work to do in the office he would have some snacks there instead of coming home for lunch.

'Master come home. He say he no want lunch because he go miss plane. Then he left with his blue box. That one he take when he want go for tour.'

'What time did he leave?'

'Madam, I no look at clock.'

Ije was puzzled. Dozie had not told her he was going on tour before she left for the clinic in the morning. Something must have cropped up while she was away. She thought it must have been very urgent otherwise he would not have left without lunch and without waiting for her to come back.

'I put food for you, madam?' James asked.

'Yes, James. See that the soup is warm.'

'Yes, madam.' He took the bottle and went to fill it from the filter in the dining-room.

Ije walked to the bedroom. The house was very quiet. If only I had a child to dispel the silence with his shrieks and laughter, she thought. She stopped by the bedroom door and turned.

'James!' she called.

'Madam?'

'Where is Teresa?'

'Madam, she say she want go tie her hair.'

'I wonder how many times a week she has her hair tied!'

James said nothing. He was now taking some plates from the sideboard.

Inside the bedroom, Ije began to undress. Then she saw a folded piece of paper on her dressing table, with her name on it. It was a note from her husband telling her that he had to leave for Port Harcourt suddenly. He had received a phone call from one of his contact men there asking him to come at once for some urgent business. He stated that he did not know when he would be back but would endeavour to come home as soon as he finished his mission there.

Ije read the note again and, putting it away in one of her drawers, she continued undressing. She took her time because there was no need to hurry. She was a simple woman by nature and rarely wore any make-up. Once, a woman had told her, a little unkindly, that she did not know how to spend her husband's money. The woman had lectured her on what she could spend money on, and had ended by condemning her lack of sophistication. But the woman's words had fallen on deaf ears because Ije had never cared for such things. Her only, obsession was to have a child and nothing else meant much to her except, of course, her husband whom she loved deeply.

'Madam, your food is ready,' James called from the sitting-room.

'All right, James,' Ije said. She was not really hungry. She disliked eating alone, and ate less when her husband was away.

A few minutes later, she sat down to a lunch of garri and okra soup. After eating she took her drugs and went to the bedroom for a rest. For some time she lay awake, her thoughts playing hide and seek with her. She remembered the argument that had gone on between two women in the clinic that day. The dispute had begun when one of the women had stated categorically that all men were unfaithful. The other woman would not agree with this assertion and a heated argument had ensued and had continued until one of the women was called in for her test.

For one split second, the idea of Dozie being unfaithful to her flickered in Ije's mind like a match flame on a windy day, and then went off leaving a smoky trail behind. Then she told herself that her thought was baseless and must have been brought about by the argument she had listened to in the clinic. She loved Dozie dearly and he had always reciprocated in spite of her inability to fulfil all her functions as a wife.

One of the drugs she had taken must have had a sedative effect, for in spite of the quibblings in her mind she soon fell into a deep slumber.

* * *

It was about six o'clock in the evening. Ije, after her refreshing sleep, was in the sitting-room eating groundnuts and popcorn when the doorbell rang. She went and opened the door.

'Patience!' she shouted as she hugged her visitor. 'When did you come back?'

Patience beamed with smiles. 'Three days ago,' she answered. 'I ran into Uju this morning. You remember Uju, don't you?'

'Yes, of course,' Ije said gaily.

'She told me about you,' Patience continued, 'and gave me your address, so I decided to call on you before going back to Lagos tomorrow.'

'That was very kind of you. Please come in. I'm so pleased to see you again since we parted years ago in London.'

When they came into the sitting-room, Ije said. 'Do sit down, Patience. It's lovely to see you.'

Patience sat down in one of the huge and cosy armchairs. In a flash her eyes took in everything in the room. She noticed that there was an air of elegance and personal pride in the furniture.

'How is Mike?' Ije inquired after sitting down. Mike was Patience's husband.

'He's fine,' Patience replied.

'It's a long time since I saw him last.'

'Well, he's still the same Mike you know,' Patience said. 'He's desperately looking for a job now. One firm in Lagos offered him a job which made him decide to leave London and his lucrative practice there. And now the Lagos firm regrets they cannot offer him the job any more.' She said the word 'regrets' with a grimace.

Ije said kindly, 'Never mind, he'll soon find another job.'

'I hope he does.'

'What can I offer you, Patience? You need something to cool you down. It is such a hot day.'

'Anything. Whisky, gin, campari, brandy. Give me anything you have. I'm jack of all trades,' she added, laughing.

Ije rang the bell and James appeared.

'Yes, madam?'

'Is Teresa not back yet?'

James scratched his head and said, 'Madam, she no come back yet. She stay long when she go tie her hair.'

'Get my friend some sherry and ice and some orange squash for me. You remember which bottle contains the sherry?'

'Yes, madam,' James affirmed and left.

'Don't tell me, Ije, that you drink only squash,' Patience said. Then she looked around her for the hundredth time. Since she had stepped into the sitting-room her eyes had been darting from one item of furniture to another.

'H'm, Ije,' Patience said. 'You must be swimming in money. Your house is expensively furnished.' There was a faint note of jealousy in her voice. The five rings on the five fingers of her left hand glittered as she smoothed her 'permed' hair with her hand.

'I won't say we are,' Ije replied in her usual modest way. 'We have just enough to feed ourselves and our dependants in the village.'

Although Ije's modesty would not allow her to agree that she and Dozie were doing well, there was no doubt about their wealth as one could see from the exquisite furnishing of their home – a three-bedroomed bungalow which they rented from a friend.

Patience's comment made Ije remember how poor she and Dozie had been when they were in England. She remembered her wedding day. It was a very quiet wedding because they had no money to invite a lot of people. She had borrowed a wedding gown from a friend. Another friend who was studying home economics had helped her make the wedding cake to save money. But those days were gone, she told herself.

'Where does your husband work now, Ije?' Patience was curious.

'He's on his own.'

'On his own?' Patience asked incredulously.

'Yes,' Ije replied calmly, taking the tray of drinks from James who had just appeared with it. She poured out some sherry for her friend and mixed herself some orange squash.

'Yes, my husband is on his own now.' Ije sat down and took a sip from her drink. 'When we came back from England he got a job as a surveyor in the Ministry and I secured a job in an insurance company.'

'That's interesting,' Patience said, looking around her with wonder mingled with envy. 'So he made all this money as a civil servant?' she asked a little maliciously. She had gulped down her sherry and Ije poured some more for her.

'There's no money in the civil service,' Ije explained. 'After my husband had been with the Ministry for three years a friend of his urged him to resign and start something on his own. You know Dozie. He finds it difficult to take decisions. When he told me about it, I advised him to resign. Excuse me, Patience.' She left the sitting-room.

Patience, now left alone, surveyed the room again with keen interest. She noticed the heavy red brocade curtains and the dainty white lace curtains that hung in between the red ones. Her eyes did not miss the big colour T.V. set and the expensive stereo set.

Presently, Ije appeared with a plate of fruit-cake.

'Would you care for a piece of cake?' she asked, setting the plate on a small stool beside her guest. She took a piece of cake from the plate and went to her chair.

Patience looked at the plate. 'Oh dear,' she cried, 'you're tempting me, Ije. I'm slimming but I won't let you take this cake away.' She took a piece of the cake and popped it into her mouth. She chewed in silence for a while and said, 'Continue your story, Ije, I'm interested.'

'Well, there's nothing much to tell, Patience. He resigned, hired an office and began working on his own. Later I resigned my job in order to help him.'

'I see,' Patience said meditatively. She took another piece of cake and popped it into her mouth. Her bulging belly, puffy cheeks and fat upper arms showed that she enjoyed food and ate more than was good for her figure.

'You're a very lucky woman, Ije,' Patience continued. 'By the way, I haven't seen your children. Are they out or sleeping?' She had been told by Uju that Ije had no children but she wanted to prove Uju right or wrong.

Ije's face suddenly became sullen. Then, bracing herself, she told Patience that no child had blessed her marriage yet.

'I'm very sorry to hear this, Ije. I am really very sorry,' Patience said in a tone that expressed more triumph than sympathy. She was pleased to discover that Ije did not have everything. It would have been just too unfair if she had, she reasoned.

'You married a year before me, Ije, didn't you?'

'Yes.'

'Although I was engaged before you.'

'Yes, you were,' Ije confirmed.

'Unlike your husband, mine wouldn't talk about a wedding until he had his degree certificate in his hands,' Patience said.

'I've gained nothing by marrying before you,' Ije lamented.

Patience tried to console her. 'Never mind, Ije, the children will come. I'm sure they will. I have five, you know. Four boys and a girl. Mike says I make the babies as if I know what he wants. They are sweet little angels and Mike adores them. My problem is that he wants more and I don't. Maybe I will have one more to please him – another girl perhaps – and then I'll put a final stop to the whole baby business. But children are wonderful. They make you feel so happy.'

Just then Teresa walked into the sitting-room.

'Good even', madam,' she said to Ije and then to Patience. Ije was very grateful to her for walking in at that moment, thereby putting a stop to Patience's inconsiderate rattling which was driving a knife into her already sore heart. She wished women would stop showing off their children to her and wondered why they could not understand that it was cruel to boast about their babies to a childless woman.

'Where have you been, Teresa?' she asked.

'To tie my hair, madam,' Teresa replied, playing nervously with her fingers. She was wearing one of Ije's discarded dresses. The light-pink coloured dress blended well with her fair skin. One would have thought she was Ije's younger sister and not her maid, judging from her healthy appearance.

'It has taken you a long time, Teresa,' Ije admonished gently.

'Yes, madam. There were many people. Three women were there before me and they had very long hair.'

'All right, Teresa, go and bring in the washing and see how many dresses you can iron tonight.'

'Yes, madam,' Teresa said and walked away, taking the empty plate and glasses with her.

'Don't tell me you keep a maid in your house, Ije?' Patience said after Teresa had shut the kitchen door behind her.

'Why not?'

'They're dangerous.'

'In what way?' Ije asked innocently.

'Don't be so naive, Ije. Haven't you heard of maids who displace their madams?'

'Oh! that. There's no fear of that with Teresa.'

'H'm. Ije, you never can tell,' Patience said with a mirthless laugh. 'Men? You never can tell about them. They are brutes. I have heard of maids who usurped the positions of the women they were supposed to serve. I warn you, send your maid away before it is too late! It's not safe to keep her.'

'Teresa is harmless,' Ije maintained.

'Harmless?' Patience sneered. 'She doesn't seem to me to be as innocent as she looks. She's dangerously beautiful – fair, plump, with a good crop of hair. H'm, if you ask me, you're asking for trouble, Ije. It is these ones who appear shy and naive that are the most dangerous. Don't say I didn't warn you.'

'I don't think there'll be any problem with Teresa. She's been with me for three years. Besides, Dozie is faithful. I trust him.'

'It's up to you, Ije.' Patience shrugged her shoulders. 'I'll be leaving for Lagos tomorrow to check whether our luggage has arrived. Thank you for the sherry and the cake.' She rose to go.

'That's nothing,' Ije said and followed her guest outside.

'Is that your car, Ije?' Patience inquired, pointing to a grey car parked under a tree in front of the house.

'Yes.'

'Posh! What make is it? It looks *very* expensive,' Patience prattled on. She looked around as if to see whether anyone was around. Then she lowered her voice. 'Ije, you know I always give advice to my friends whether they ask for it or not. I hope you're not one of those foolish women who say that what belongs to their husbands belongs to them too. I mean those women who don't believe in having their own separate bank accounts and investments. I do hope you're not one of them. I hope you're wise enough to put away some money for yourself while Dozie's business is booming.'

'But he's always generous to me. He never denies me anything. We do not discriminate in anything.'

'Yes, now. But what about the future? It may not always be so, Ije, and by the time you realise this it will be too late. Take my advice and put away some of the money your husband is making now in your own name. Just in case. Well, you know what I mean.'

'I'll think about it,' Ije said in a bid to put an end to the matter. She knew within her that she would never heed such advice which was necessary only where there was no love and trust between husband and wife.

'Goodbye, Ije, and thanks for your hospitality. Give my regards to Dozie when he comes back.'

'I will,' Ije said. 'And say "hello" to Mike for me. I'd like to see him again after so many years.'

Ije watched her guest drive away and breathed a sigh of relief. As she walked back into the house, she wondered why there was so much injustice in the world.

Chapter Four

Ije had just finished her supper when the doorbell rang. When James opened the door, Ugo Ushie, Ije's best friend, walked in.

'Welcome, Ugo,' Ije said, embracing her. 'How are Ayo and the children?'

'They're fine,' Ugo Ushie replied, sitting down. 'I made up my mind I must come and see you today no matter how late. Has Dozie gone to bed?'

'No,' Ije said. 'He's gone suddenly to Port Harcourt.'

'On business?'

'Yes. I didn't know he was going. I came back from the hospital to see his note telling me he has gone to Port Harcourt.'

'So you're a grass widow once again?' Ugo Ushie said with a smile.

'So I am, my dear.'

Ugo and Ije had known each other since they were ten years old. Their parents had lived in the same house in Makurdi when they were girls. Later, both of them had attended the same secondary school – a renowned one near

Port Harcourt – and had left the school at the same time. While Ugo went to a teachers' training college at Umuahia, Ije had gone overseas to do a course in accountancy. They had continued their friendship by correspondence when Ije was in England, and later, years after, both of them had settled down at Enugu as married women. To Ije, Ugo Ushie was the only real friend she had – the only woman she could confide in.

'How are the children, Ugo?' Ije asked again. 'I've not seen them for days.'

'They're fine, though U-U has a bad cough. I'm not taking him to the hospital this time. I'll treat him myself. Going to hospital these days is a whole day's affair and sometimes two.' 'U-U' was her youngest child.

'You're right,' Ije agreed. 'Unless, of course, you know any of the doctors or nurses personally.'

'Did you go to see Dr Melie as planned, Ije?'

'Yes, I did.'

'What did he say?'

'Nothing. I went through the same routine – a barrage of questions, prescription of tests, and then of course a fat bill. Let me just hope he'll be the one to find out what is wrong with me.'

'He will, I'm sure of that,' Ugo Ushie consoled her. 'He's the talk of the town. Everybody says he's extremely good. I've talked with two women whom he's treated successfully.'

Ije said sadly, 'The same has been said about those doctors who treated me before, but what could they do for me? Nothing.'

'I'm sure Dr Melie will do something for you, Ije. You worry a lot and worrying, you know as well as I do, will not improve your condition. Rather it will make it worse.'

'I can't help worrying,' Ije confessed. 'It is not easy for me to take my mind off my misfortune.' She became thoughtful for a while. 'Oh dear,' she cried, 'What a woman I am. I'm so full of my own problems, I've not offered you anything, Ugo. Get you some soft drink?'

'No, I'm quite full. We had my favourite food for supper – breadfruit and corn.'

'That's my favourite, too,' Ije said.

'By the way, Ije, somebody told me she saw Patience Odoh in town to-day. You remember her, don't you?'

'Of course I do. Patience is not the type one forgets easily. In fact she called to see me some hours ago.'

'You don't mean it!' Ugo Ushie cried, her large beautiful eyes bulging with surprise. 'How did she find out where you live?'

'She said she ran into Uju and she told her about me.' Uju was a classmate of theirs in the grammar school near Port Harcourt.

'Has she changed? Patience, I mean?'

'Changed?' Ije asked with a smile. 'Not a bit. Do you think she'll ever change? She's the same weaver-bird.'

She remained silent for a moment and then continued in a changed tone, 'She talked about her five lovely children. She asked me to send Teresa away because she's not safe with Dozie. Oh dear, she said a lot of things. She talked so much I wished I could shout at her to stop.'

'Why didn't you show her the way out?' Ugo Ushie asked without expecting an answer. 'You're too good-natured and modest for my liking, Ije. I wish I had been here to shut her up.'

Ugo Ushie was an outspoken woman who would not let anyone bully her or disparage her and get away with it. Ije, on the other hand, was different. She disliked scenes and would endure rudeness, even insults, without breathing a word.

'Imagine the bitch telling you to send Teresa away!' Ugo Ushie said with disgust. 'Imagine her gloating to you about her lovely children and all that!'

'It's not her fault that I have no children of my own,' Ije said, trying to exculpate Patience of all blame. 'Rather it's my fault that I have not learnt to accept my fate after all these years. I shouldn't moan when other women talk about their children. They have every right to do so.'

Ugo Ushie could detect the glitter of tears in her friend's eyes. She tactfully changed the topic of their conversation.

'Mrs Okoh came to see me this evening,' she said. 'She tried to talk me into joining their social club.'

Ije roared with laughter.

'Why are you laughing?'

'I can't imagine you as a member of Mrs Okoh's club,' Ije said, still laughing.

'Why not?'

'Of course you know why, Ugo! I can't imagine *you* dressing as flamboyantly as the other club members. I can't imagine *you* racing up and down our bad roads to attend the club's numerous meetings and induction ceremonies. I can't imagine *you* taking part in their gossip and backbiting. I can't imagine you doing a host of other things the club members do.'

'You're right, Ije. I can't fit in in any way. I told Mrs Okoh that I can't afford their two-hundred naira enrolment fee just to put her off.'

'And what did she say?'

'She volunteered to pay half of the fee for me!'

'And so you agreed to join the club?'

'How could I? Our people say that if a man does not know his rank, his distracters will carry him away from his homestead. I told her I can't even pay the other half, neither can I meet their other financial obligations. Do you know a member has to pay a fifty-naira fine each time she fails to attend any of their meetings, frolics and funeral ceremonies?'

'Of course I know about all those,' said Ije. 'And have you forgotten you have to attend each of these gatherings in a new "george" and lace blouse or you'll be made miserable?'

Ugo Ushie kept a straight face. 'I can't resort to what some of the women do – buy jewellery, laces and such things on credit.'

'And spend sleepless nights wondering how to pay your debts,' Ije concluded for her. 'You're just not the type, Ugo.'

'My dear, I'm not, to be frank,' Ugo agreed. 'We've all got our priorities wrong in this country, especially we women.'

'You're right, Ugo.'

'I don't know how these fashion-conscious women make both ends meet,' Ugo Ushie said, 'with the cost of living rising in leaps and bounds every day.'

The two friends talked about the hyperinflation in the country and ended by agreeing to buy a goat jointly at the end of the month and share the meat. By doing so they would save some money – the profit the butcher would have made by buying the goat, slaughtering it and selling the meat to them.

Next they watched an interesting play on the T.V., performed by a group based in Benin. Ije recognised one of the members of the cast and made a mental note to congratulate her when she saw her. When the play ended Ugo went home.

Early the next morning Ije left again for Dr Melie's clinic for the X-rays. Five uneventful days crawled by. On the sixth day she went to the clinic to collect the results of her tests and to see her doctor.

First she went to the X-ray department and collected the films and the reports. She stopped by the corner of the building to read the reports before taking them to her doctor. She knew it was wrong to read the reports which were addressed to Dr Melie, but her curiosity overcame her sense of decorum. The reports indicated that her fallopian tubes and uterus were normal. Her heart sank. She had hoped the X-rays would show that something was wrong with her so that when this was corrected she would be able to have her babies.

When she collected the reports of the urine and blood tests she tried to read them but could not make head nor tail of them. She hoped that these reports would be the ones to show the doctor what was wrong with her.

She knocked lightly on the door which was used by Dr Melie's special patients, and opened it without waiting for an answer. She peeped in.

'Good morning, doctor,' she greeted him.

'Good morning, Mrs Apia, I'll see you in a few minutes,' said the doctor.

'Right, doctor,' Ije said, closing the door noiselessly. She waited patiently for Dr Melie to finish with the patient sitting in front of him. A few minutes later, the nurse called her in.

'Are the results of the tests ready?' the doctor asked her.

Ije nodded and handed him the X-ray films and the

reports. She watched him carefully as he read the reports, hoping to detect something from his countenance. But Dr Melie's face remained expressionless.

'Well, young lady,' he said after reading the reports, 'I'll give you some drugs that will last you for six weeks. Come and see me after that and maybe you'll have something pleasant to tell me.'

He began to fold the reports. Ije wanted to ask him what was wrong with her. Then she changed her mind. What was the use? It was not that she believed that ignorance was bliss, but that she suspected that Dr Melie would not be willing to tell her.

On the way home she stopped at Ugo Ushie's school to tell her the result of her visit to the clinic. They talked for about a quarter of an hour outside Ugo Ushie's classroom. When Ugo Ushie espied her headmistress come out of her office, she hurriedly bade her friend goodbye and tiptoed back into her classroom.

Dozie came home from Port Harcourt late in the evening. Ije was very happy to have him home again. She hugged him affectionately.

'Welcome, D.,' she said. 'James! Come and bring in Master's box!'

James appeared almost immediately and took the box. Dozie and Ije walked behind him.

'But, D., why didn't you telephone me to come and fetch you back from the airport instead of taking a taxi?'

'I didn't want to bother you unnecessarily,' Dozie said, following Ije into the sitting-room. 'Besides it was quicker taking a taxi. And how is my Ije?' he ended fondly.

'Fine. Only I missed you greatly.'

'I did, too. I'm very sorry I had to leave without prior notice. I had no alternative.'

'It's all right. I understand. I saw your note when I came back from the hospital.'

'Have you finished with the tests?' Dozie asked.

'Yes.'

'And you've seen the doctor since then? What did he say?'

'I'll tell you everything after you've changed and eaten.' They met James coming out of the bedroom where he had deposited Dozie's box.

'Get food ready for Master, James,' Ije instructed.

'Yes, madam.'

'And be quick about it, James. There's some soup in a white bowl in the fridge. Warm it and make some garri. Don't put too much water in the garri. And don't add any water at all to the soup. Leave it as thick as it is.'

'Yes, madam,' James said and walked into the kitchen.

Ije did most of the cooking herself, leaving little chores like warming soup, making garri, and preparing the ingredients to James. Teresa was responsible for the laundry and the general cleanliness of the house.

Ije followed her husband into the bedroom and while he undressed, she ran his bath-water for him. Her friends had often railed at her for doting on her husband. But she would not be daunted. She loved Dozie dearly and it annoyed her greatly to hear men say that African women were incapable of deep love for their husbands.

When Dozie entered the bathroom, Ije went to the kitchen to see to his food. James was a reliable aide. All the same she wanted to make sure that everything was all right.

A few minutes later, Dozie settled down to a good meal.

'Won't you have some more?' he asked Ije.

'No. It's not long since I had lunch.'

'Now tell me the results of your tests at Dr Melie's.'

'When you've finished your food,' Ije said.

Dozie ate ravenously. He liked good food and would not listen to any preaching about slimming. He was becoming a little overweight but he did not care.

'This is the first time I've eaten good food since I left you about six days ago,' Dozie said. 'Hotel food in Nigeria is horrible! I'll never get used to it, I'm sure.'

He ate as he talked. In no time he had consumed a big plate of garri. Ije watched him take the last piece of garri. After he had swallowed it, he began to scoop the remaining soup into his mouth with his fingers, licking the fingers as little children do. When the soup plate was clean, he belched satisfactorily. Ije called Teresa to clear the table.

While Dozie rested in bed, Ije told him about her visits to Dr Melie's clinic while he was away. Dozie listened carefully, asking only a few questions. Ije ended her report on a sad note. Dozie comforted her and tactfully changed the subject.

He said, 'A friend in Port Harcourt is helping me get a contract for designing a hotel there.'

'Can you do that alone?' Ije wondered aloud.

'I don't think I can. If I get the contract, I'll have to get help overseas. If I succeed in winning the contract we'll be swimming in money.'

'I hope you do get it. You deserve it. You work so hard.'

'Before the end of the week, I may get a cheque for the plans I designed for the new Agricultural Institute. You remember you suggested we buy a piece of land with the money?'

'I still think that's a good idea, or have you changed your mind?'

Dozie shook his head. 'No. Tomorrow we'll go and look at three pieces of land. You'll help me choose the one that will be best for us.'

'Where are they?' Ije asked.

'One is in New Haven, another is in G.R.A. The third is in Independence Layout.'

'I already know where my preference lies,' Ije declared. 'I'll wait and see the sites first, anyway.'

* * *

After supper, Dozie and Ije sat on the balcony of their house enjoying the cool night breeze. As usual NEPA had put their part of the town into darkness. The moon, a silver bow in the sky, gave out a faint light.

A car drove into the drive-way throwing its headlights momentarily on them.

'That must be David,' Dozie said. 'He has a peculiar way of driving into these premises.' David was his friend. He was a civil servant, who had been with him in the Ministry before he resigned to be on his own.

The car screeched to a halt in front of the house. A man emerged from it and walked towards them. Dozie was right. It was David.

'Hello, lovebirds!' David said. 'Having a cuddling session? I hope I am not intruding.'

'Yes, David, you are, so better go back,' Dozie said, chuckling.

'Good evening, David,' Ije greeted. 'How's Emily?' Emily was his wife. Although David and Dozie were the best of friends, their wives did not get on well. They were incompatible. Emily was as sophisticated as Ije was simple. Twice David had complained in Ije's hearing that Emily was too expensive for him. Emily and David had three children, however.

Dozie rang the bell and James appeared. He told him to bring a chair for David.

'A beer, David?' Dozie asked his friend after he had sat down.

'Of course,' David said. 'Have you ever heard me refuse beer?'

'I thought you might for a change,' Dozie said, chuckling. He instructed James to bring a bottle of beer for David and one for him.

When the two men settled down to their beer, Ije disappeared into the house. A few minutes later, she came out with two plates of steaming *ngwo-ngwo* for her husband and David.

David took the plate from Ije gratefully. His sophisticated wife was always out looking for contracts and so had no time for such delicacies. He stuffed his mouth with a spoonful of the pepper-soup.

'This goat-meat is delicious,' he said. 'Aren't you lucky, Dozie, to have such a wife as Ije?'

'Don't flatter me now, David,' Ije protested, smiling.

'I mean what I've said,' David affirmed, 'and I don't mind saying it in your presence. You're a big asset and Dozie knows it. Don't you, Dozie?'

'Too well,' Dozie said. 'I owe my success in my business venture to her. I don't know what I would have done without her.'

David had known the Apias in London. He had not forgotten how Ije had worked at two jobs at a time in order to help Dozie pay his way through the university. Whenever a man said in his presence that Nigerian women were no good he remembered Ije and her devotion.

Soon Dozie and David settled down to another bottle of beer each. Ije left them and retired into the house. By the time Dozie had come in she was fast asleep.

Chapter Five

The following evening Dozie and Ije went to look at the pieces of land for sale. They got into Dozie's car and Ije took the wheel as she often did when he was tired.

'Which land are we seeing first?' Ije asked. She was guiding the car round a sharp turn and over a path into the main street.

Dozie became thoughtful. 'Let's go to New Haven first,' he suggested. 'We'll go to Independence Layout after that.'

'And the G.R.A. one last,' Ije added.

'Yes, the nearest one last,' Dozie agreed.

After they had seen the three pieces of land, they agreed to buy the one in Independence Layout. It was situated in the best place. The owner of this land demanded a large sum of money for it, but Dozie was in the position to pay. He got David to check the man's claim to the land from the Ministry of Lands, and when this was ascertained, he engaged a lawyer to draw up an agreement between him and the owner of the piece of land. A few days later, he was the proud owner of a large plot in Independence Layout.

For days the Apias discussed their dream house. They looked at books on houses, and considered what they liked in other houses they had been into. From all these they arrived at the design of their own house.

Once the decision was taken, Dozie began the architectural work of the house. He sought Ije's opinion now and again on some aspects of the house. During this time he made more trips to Port Harcourt in a bid to get the contract for designing a hotel.

One afternoon Dozie and Ije came back to see Gabriel waiting for them in the house. Gabriel was the lad who lived with Dozie's mother in the village.

'Is anything wrong at home, Gabriel?' Dozie asked.

'No, sir,' Gabriel replied.

A look of relief passed over Dozie's face.

'Is Mama all right?' he inquired.

'Yes, sir. She sent me to you. She said you and madam should come home with me.'

Dozie asked, 'Are you sure nothing is wrong with Mama?'

'Nothing, sir. I swear to God. Mama is fine,' Gabriel declared.

Dozie turned to Ije who had been standing near him without saying a word.

'Well, Ije, we can't go to see Mama today. It's already late. We'll leave early tomorrow morning.'

'In which case I'll go to the market now and buy foodstuffs for Mama,' Ije suggested.

'That's a good idea,' agreed Dozie.

They sat down to a late lunch after which Ije left for the market and Dozie went back to his office to finish the work he had on hand.

The next day was Saturday. Dozie, Ije and Gabriel left for the village after breakfast. Throughout the journey, Ije thought about Mama and why she wanted to see Dozie, her only surviving son. There had been two other sons besides Dozie but both of them had died before they were old enough to marry. Dozie's father had died when Dozie was in England.

An hour's drive brought them to the village. It was a market day and many villagers had left for the market. But Mama was there waiting for them. Dozie heaved a sigh of relief when he saw his mother looking so well. Mama welcomed him affectionately, but from the way she replied to Ije's warm greetings, one could see that a coldness existed between her and her daughter-in-law.

Ije, a good-natured woman by any standard, had tried her best to bring the cold war between her and Mama to an end, but had not succeeded. She gave Mama the foodstuffs she had brought for her, although she knew from experience that she would receive little or no gratitude for her trouble.

'Is anything wrong at home, Mama?' Dozie asked.

'At least nobody has died,' Mama said. 'Your uncles want to talk to you.'

'Which ones? Your brothers?'

'No, Dozie. It's your father's brothers who have asked me to send for you.'

'What do they want to talk to me about, Mama?' Dozie asked curiously.

Mama declared, 'You'll soon know what it is all about. But first you'll have some food. Your uncles have gone to market. They'll be back in no time.'

Dozie was bent on finding out beforehand why his uncles wanted him.

He asked, 'Mama, can't you give me a hint before my uncles are back? I need to be prepared before meeting them.'

'There's no need to be in a hurry, Dozie,' Mama said dogmatically. 'You'll know soon enough what it is all about. Let me get your food now.'

Mama left Dozie and Ije in the main house and went into her kitchen, a little hut behind the house. A little later, Ije went into the kitchen to help her but she turned down her help a little unkindly. All the same Ije did not leave the kitchen. She sat down on a low stool and watched her mother-in-law warm the bitter-leaf soup she had made specially for her son, while Gabriel pounded the yam for *foo-foo*.

Mama had opposed her son's marriage to Ije from the outset. When Dozie had written to her from England telling her he had found a girl to marry, she had written back forbidding the marriage. She got her letter-writer to state her reasons for opposing the marriage carefully: highly educated girls were in most cases wayward and often childless, they were also headstrong and disrespectful. Mama had also feared that Ije might be an *Osu*.

Dozie had written back extolling Ije's merits and assuring his mother that Ije was neither an *Osu* nor a tart. Mama would not be won over by her son's praises of Ije, but in spite of her opposition, Dozie went ahead and married Ije.

When, a year after coming home, Ije was still without a child, Mama had gloried in her vindication.

'I knew it! I told you so!' she had said one day to Dozie in Ije's hearing.

But Dozie had come to Ije's defence at once. He had stated that it was too early to brand Ije a barren woman. She had to get used to the new environment and to her new job. Mama was not convinced, and as the years passed without Ije becoming pregnant, Dozie had stopped giving reasons for her childlessness.

Gabriel served Dozie and Ije their lunch in the main house while Mama ate her own in the kitchen. When lunch was over, Mama called her son and daughter-in-law into her kitchen. She did not waste time in telling them why she had called them.

'Now that you're here,' she said to Dozie, 'let me take your wife to a herbalist at Nze. That's after you've been to see your uncles. This herbalist is very good, they say. I don't know why I had not thought about him before all these years.'

Dozie and Ije remained silent. Mama continued, 'Nze is not far from here. We'll be able to come back before sunset.'

Dozie and Ije said nothing. Ije always liked to remain in the background when Dozie and Mama were discussing anything. She remembered with a shudder the ordeal she had gone through when Mama took her to a herbalist a year or so before. The herbalist had given her a purgative for a start, so powerful that her stomach had run for two days without stop. When she was on the verge of collapse, her uncle-in-law had chartered a taxi to rush her back to Enugu. She had narrowly escaped death and Dozie had not forgiven himself for leaving Ije behind for the herbalist's treatment.

'Dozie!' Mama said, bringing Ije back to the present. 'Didn't you hear me?'

'I heard you, Mama.'

'Then what is there to think about? Don't you want me to have a grandchild? What is wrong in going to a herbalist?'

Dozie was again silent. Ije had by now made up her mind not to go with Mama to see any herbalist that day. The last experience was still very green in her memory. She might have lost her life just because she had been afraid to offend her mother-in-law by refusing to see the herbalist. This time she was not afraid of her any longer.

Dozie seemed to read Ije's mind.

'Mama,' he said, 'Ije is having some treatment right

now. It will not be safe for her to take two different kinds of treatment at the same time.'

'Who's giving her the treatment?' Mama asked. The contempt in her voice was glaring.

'A doctor at Enugu,' Dozie replied.

'Are you not tired of those doctors of yours? What have they done for you after all these years? What have they done for you? Tell me!'

Dozie did not want to argue with his mother for fear of her hysterical outbursts of fury. Besides, she hardly ever listened to argument. She was a domineering woman. When her husband was alive, it was she who ruled the house. Her husband was a man of few words who hated scenes and who, many a time, had allowed her to have her way if only to have some peace in the house.

'Yes, I knew all along you would say no to my suggestion,' Mama continued. 'Your wife will not like to go to see the herbalist so you support her. I saw her give you a sign with her eyes. Whoever denies me the opportunity to have a grandchild will meet with misfortune all her life!'

Mama's temper was rising. Dozie tried to quieten her, but his attempts were like pouring kerosene into an already blazing fire. She became vituperative. She called her daughter-in-law all sorts of derogatory names. She said her childlessness was a punishment for her unchaste life as a spinster.

Ije did not say a word. It grieved her to see that Dozie

was so helpless that he could not restrain his mother from casting such aspersions upon her integrity. Nothing was worse in her position than the consciousness of her innocence. It undermined her morale. It was on the tip of her tongue to exculpate herself. She could feel her temper rising – the familiar pressure in the chest and the choking feeling in the throat – but she controlled herself and allowed Mama to go on and vent her spleen.

Dozie was speechless too. He stared at his mother in consternation. If only people would leave him and Ije alone to solve their own problems by themselves, he thought.

At last, when Mama had nothing more to say, she burst into tears. Ije moved over to her and began to console her, even though she, too, was on the verge of crying.

'Mama,' she said, putting her hand on her mother-in-law's lap, 'a child comes from God. I still believe that one day God will give you many grandchildren through me. I lived a pure life as a girl. Only God is my witness.' There were tears in her voice.

'It's all right, Ije,' Dozie said, finding his tongue. 'Mama, I am taking Ije to Enugu. If, when she finishes with the treatment she's having now, nothing happens, I'll bring her home for you to take her to this herbalist. Will that be all right?'

'As you say,' Mama agreed. She was now spent. She looked helpless and Ije felt sorry for her, for Dozie, and for her unfortunate self, too.

Soon Dozie's paternal uncles came back from the

market and sent for him. He went alone to see them for he had guessed why they wanted him. His guess was correct. Without mincing their words his uncles told him it was high time he took a second wife to give him an heir. They spoke of his mother's unhappiness and ended by telling him that certain events he would not understand showed that his father was also unhappy in his grave.

Dozie heard them out without a word. Then he said gravely, 'Thank you for your concern. I'll go back to Enugu and think over your advice.'

Dozie and Ije left for Enugu that same day, a little before five o'clock in the evening. They had planned to pass the night in the village and go home the next day which was Sunday, but the events of the day had made the atmosphere too grim for them to stay.

Dozie drove the car by instinct. He was deep in thought most of the time. Ije was as reticent as ever. All through the journey she thought about what Mama had said to her. She tried to put herself in Mama's position, to see the whole situation through Mama's eyes. But she found it difficult to forgive Mama for calumniating her even though her anxiety might be justified. She wanted to ask Dozie some questions, to ask him for some explanations, but when she saw how he sat behind the wheel distraught with grief, she decided to wait until they got home.

They arrived at Enugu just before dusk. Dozie, looking tired and moody, said he did not want any supper and went straight to bed. Ije was too bemused by the events of the day to think about food. She sat alone in the sitting-room long after Dozie had gone to bed, while multitudes of emotions churned her mind. At midnight she went to bed.

About two weeks after the unhappy trip to the village, Dozie received a phone call from his contact man in Port Harcourt telling him to come at once. Dozie wanted Ije to go with him, but she declined the offer saying it was not safe for her to travel at that time of her monthly cycle.

The next day, Dozie left for Port Harcourt. Ije saw him to the car and bade him safe journey.

'I'll keep my fingers crossed for you, Ije,' Dozie said as his newly employed driver let in the clutch.

Ije merely smiled and watched the car until it disappeared at the end of the street.

The morning hours crawled. Teresa left for market, and James, having finished his morning chores, retired to the boys' quarters. Ije felt very lonely. The silence in the house was almost unbearable. She decided to play some music to dispel the eerie stillness. She lay awake till lunch time and after eating she went to bed again for she had decided to have as much rest as she could.

When she woke up from her siesta, it was already five o'clock in the evening. She took a shower, changed into a beautiful 'Accra' wrapper and blouse and went into the sitting-room.

'Teresa!' she called.

'Yes, madam?' Teresa answered from the kitchen.

'Is James there?'

'No, madam,' Teresa replied as she came into the sitting-room. Her hands were wet from washing plates and she tried to dry them with her dress.

'Teresa, I've told you not to do that,' Ije reprimanded her. 'There's a towel for drying hands in the kitchen, isn't there?'

'Sorry, madam, I forgot,' Teresa apologised.

'Where is James?' Ije asked.

'Out.'

'Where?'

'I don't know, madam.'

'When he comes back tell him we'll have beans for supper. Tell him to use some of the cooked meat in the fridge.'

'Yes, madam.'

'And lock the front door when I go out and stay in the house until James comes back. There are many thieves around these days.'

'Yes, madam.'

'I'm going to see Mrs Ushie. I'll be back before supper,' Ije said.

She went out of the house and waited until she heard Teresa bolt and lock the door. Then she got into her car and drove off.

On her way to the Ushies', she stopped at a small supermarket and bought two packets of biscuits, a packet of sweets, and some cones of ice-cream for Ugo Ushie's children. A few minutes' drive brought her to Ugo Ushie's flat. She parked her car in the street. U-U, the youngest of Ugo Ushie's children, was the first to see her.

'Auntie, auntie!' he cried, running to meet her. He tripped and nearly fell. Ije rushed forward and scooped him up just in time.

U-U's shout of joy brought Ugo Ushie to the scene.

'Auntie, did you bring anything for me?' U-U asked, tugging at Ije's handbag.

'Stop that, U-U,' Ugo Ushie reprimanded her son before Ije could answer his question.

'That's enough, Ugo.' It was now Ije's turn to reprimand her friend. She turned to U-U who had been momentarily put off by his mother's harsh words. 'I've brought you something, U-U,' she said to him, 'but fetch your sisters first.'

U-U dashed off. The women smiled after him. Ugo Ushie shook her head.

'U-U is a big case, a very big one,' she said as she led the way into her sitting-room. 'And how you love to spoil them, Ije!'

The women were hardly seated when the Ushie daughters, led by their brother, ran in. Shouts of 'Auntie, Auntie!' rang through the air. They all crowded round Ije as she distributed the biscuits, sweets and ice-cream.

The Ushies had four children. The eldest daughter, Angy, was about ten. A boy born before her had died of convulsions just before he was two. Angy was a beautiful girl – a carbon-copy of her mother. There were two other girls, Ezinma and Oche. They were as fair as their mother but had their father's broad face and not too handsome a nose. U-U, the only boy, also had some of his mother's beautiful features. Ugo Ushie had often said that God had originally made U-U a girl but had changed his mind at the last minute to please her. U-U was a handsome little boy, plump and dark-skinned, with smiling eyes and one dimple on each cheek. Ije loved him best of all the Ushie children.

'Now run out and play,' Ugo Ushie shouted at her children. 'I haven't heard you say "thank you" nicely.'

'Thank you, Auntie,' the children shouted together and ran off happily.

Ije became sad for a fleeting second. If only God would give her one of such lively healthy and happy children!

'Let me get you some squash, Ije,' Ugo Ushie said, rising from her chair.

Ije said, 'I don't mind. It's hot and I feel thirsty.'

The two friends were sipping their drinks and chatting animatedly when Ayo Ushie returned from the Sports Club where he had been to play tennis.

'Hello, Ije,' he said to Ije. 'How are you?'

'Fine. And you?' Ije said.

'Not so fine, your friend Ugo doesn't look after me so well these days, or do you?' He turned to his wife with a chuckle.

Ugo Ushie smiled at her husband.

'Men who tell lies do not grow beard,' she declared humorously.

'So our people say,' Ayo Ushie agreed. 'I don't grow beard and I am not a liar.' He took his wife's glass and drained it. 'You grow beard when you are well fed, not when you are starved,' he added humorously, and left the women to themselves. Just before seven o'clock, Ije left the Ushies' for home.

She had a late supper, and feeling out of sorts, she went straight to bed. She slept very badly, waking up intermittently and sleeping off again after some minutes of wakefulness. Occasionally she felt a slight pain in the small of her back.

At about five-thirty in the morning the cause of her discomfort manifested itself. This month of all months she had thought that her wish for a child of her own would be granted her. Early in the month she had had a dream in which a beautiful bonny boy was being handed over to her from the skies, she could not see the person presenting the baby to her but could only see a pair of hands. In the dream she had taken the baby thankfully. She had become sad when she discovered that the whole thing was a dream.

For days after this dream she had imagined herself sitting in front of Dr Melie and telling him with broad smiles that she had started a baby. For days she had imagined

Dozie's joy on being told he would be a father after all. Now all these hopes were dashed as the pain in her back continued to remind her.

Crestfallen, she confined herself to her bedroom and gave instructions to Teresa that she would not see anyone.

Chapter Six

Six months had now passed since Ije paid her first visit to Dr Melie's clinic and yet there was no change in her. As the months came and went in quick succession, she became more and more despondent, and more so when she noticed that most of the women who had been attending the clinic with her were now expecting babies.

Dozie was aware of Ije's despondency. He, too, was feeling crestfallen. His hopes had risen with Ije's when they were first told of Dr Melie and his expertise. Now to both of them Dr Melie was gradually joining the host of those doctors who could do nothing for them.

'Next summer you'll go overseas for treatment,' Dozie suggested to Ije one evening. 'I am sure the doctors there will discover where the trouble with you lies.'

Ije welcomed the suggestion gladly. Summer was still months away, but what did it matter? She had waited for a child for years without success, why then could she not wait for a few months more?

'Meanwhile,' Dozie continued, 'why not write to one of

your friends in London to get you an appointment with a good doctor?'

'I'll write the letter tomorrow,' Ije declared with fresh enthusiasm. 'The best doctors are usually fully booked in summer so the earlier I write the surer I'll be of getting an appointment.'

Two days after this conversation, Beatrice Ilodi paid Ije a surprise visit. Dozie and Ije were in the sitting-room eating fresh tapioca and coconut when Beatrice walked in. She was noticeably pregnant and looking very well. Ije had not seen her in Dr Melie's clinic for months and had been wondering what had happened to her.

'Where have you been all these weeks, Beatrice?' Ije exclaimed.

'In Enugu,' Beatrice said, laughing.

'I don't believe you – I've not seen you in the clinic for months.'

'I've stopped going there.'

'Why?'

'It's a long story,' Beatrice replied.

Ije introduced Beatrice to Dozie as her 'clinic friend' and offered her some of the tapioca.

'What can I get you, beer or soft drink?' Ije asked Beatrice.

'Have you a small bottle of stout?'

'Yes. I think I have.'

'Then let me have stout,' Beatrice said and reclined on her chair.

Ije left to get the stout. She was itching to ask Beatrice who had performed the 'miracle' on her. Presently she was back with a small bottle of stout. She served Beatrice and asked Dozie if he wanted a beer.

'No, not now,' Dozie replied. 'And I think I'd better leave you ladies alone. That will give you the freedom to gossip.' He said the last word with a chuckle.

'You can gossip with us,' Beatrice said, smiling, as Dozie stood up to go. She was a happy woman by nature and her present condition had made her even happier.

'Next time I'll gossip with you,' Dozie said and left the sitting-room.

'Congratulations!' Ije said to Beatrice as soon as Dozie was out of hearing. 'What really happened to you, Beatrice? After some time I stopped seeing you in Dr Melie's clinic. I didn't know who to ask about you.'

Beatrice took a sip from her drink. 'I attended Dr Melie's clinic for about two months. After that I switched over to a faith healer whose church is near my house. I told you I would if Dr Melie failed me, didn't I?'

'You did,' Ije admitted.

'I need not tell you that the faith healer succeeded where the doctors had failed,' Beatrice declared triumphantly. 'I'm four and a half months gone.'

'What a lucky woman you are, Beatrice. I am very happy for you.'

'Are you still attending Dr Melie's clinic?' Beatrice asked.

'Yes, I am. But quite frankly I think there's nothing more he can do for me.'

Beatrice shifted in her chair. 'As a matter of fact I've come to tell you about this faith healer,' she said. 'Maybe you'd like to give him a trial, too.'

Ije listened attentively to her friend's tale of success, then she said, 'I'll talk this over with my husband first.'

Beatrice was surprised. 'Do you have to talk it over with him first?' she asked.

'Of course, I can't do anything without telling him about it first. Not that he insists that I do, but I like confiding in him just as he likes confiding in me, too.'

Beatrice shrugged her shoulders. 'Well, I'm different,' she said. 'I don't always tell my husband about all my actions. I have my secrets. I'm sure my husband has his. You know what men are! You can't trust them out of your sight so why should they be told everything by their wives?'

Ije did not comment on these views. She did not accept them but she left it at that. She had given her whole life to her husband, always taking him into her confidence and she had never regretted doing so. Reciprocally, Dozie's love for his wife was noteworthy; a love that had been ennobled by the fact that Ije had married him when he had no material wealth to offer her.

'When will you let me know if you'd like to see the faith-healer?' Beatrice asked Ije.

'Tomorrow evening, perhaps,' Ije replied, and Beatrice told her where to find her.

After Beatrice had gone, Ije sat for a long time thinking over her suggestion. She did not think much of faith-healers. In fact she had looked down on them and had talked about them with contempt. Now she found it difficult to swallow her words. But her desire for a child was so great that it had always made nonsense of both her religious faith and her reason.

Later that same day she told Dozie about Beatrice's suggestion that she should give the faith-healer, who had treated her successfully, a trial.

Dozie was sceptical. 'What will this faith-healer do for you?' he asked.

'Beatrice says he'll pray for me and will tell me what to do in order to propitiate God.'

'But we've decided that you'll go overseas for treatment in the summer,' Dozie reminded her.

'Summer is still months away,' Ije stated. 'If I succeed with the faith-healer, there'll be no need for me to go to England again.'

Dozie became thoughtful. He had always believed that the faith-healers' claims of success where doctors had failed were spurious, but he did not want to dampen his wife's spirits. Besides, he reasoned, there might be one or two genuine faith-healers.

'I have no objection, Ije,' he said at last. 'You know I'm

dying to have you bear my children. I'll sanction anything that will make our dreams come true.'

The next day was Saturday and towards evening, Ije called at Beatrice's house to inform her of her decision to see the faith-healer. Beatrice was away and so also was her husband. Ije therefore left a note for Beatrice telling her she would be ready to go to the faith-healer's church with her on Sunday.

Just as Ije was about to drive away she caught sight of Beatrice walking home. She waited for her.

'I was just about to go,' Ije said. 'I've left you a note telling you I'd like to see the faith-healer.'

'I'm very happy to hear that, Ije. Let's go back to the house. This is the first time you're visiting me.'

Ije followed Beatrice back to her house, and was lavishly entertained. Beatrice treated her like a very dear friend, although they had met only four times before, three in Dr Melie's clinic and once in Ije's house. Beatrice might be garrulous, but her kindness was enough to compensate for all her faults.

The faith-healer's church was an unfinished building in a densely populated part of the town. Ije was dressed in the uniform of the members of the faith-healer's church: a long white gown (hurriedly made the day before) and a white head-dress. She and Beatrice, who were a few minutes early, sat on a form at the back of the church.

Gradually, the church began to fill up. Ije watched the members troop in barefoot, carrying their shoes with them and depositing them beside their seats. Beatrice had told her earlier, when she was enumerating the rules of the church for her, that members used to leave their footwear outside until a rogue made away with some of the shoes while their owners were at prayer.

At eight o'clock, the faith-healer, Apostle Joseph, came into the church. He was dressed in a long red robe, a small white cap and a deep blue sash. His hair was as tangled as that of a *dada* and his beard as long as that of an *Ayotollah*. Immediately he walked into the church he began an incantation which reminded Ije of one of the herbalists who had treated her. All of a sudden, the congregation became charged as if with electricity and they began to sing and dance as though possessed. The service was in full swing.

Ije remained passive throughout because she did not know the hymns nor the responses. Besides, she was shy by nature and was never a good dancer. She watched transfixed as the congregation were carried away by the emotive words of the hymns.

Towards the end of the service, Apostle Joseph announced that the new converts should come up one after the other to the altar to give offerings to God and to be prayed for. Ije was not taken unawares by this announcement because Beatrice had briefed her well and she had put some money in an envelope for the offering.

The first new convert to walk up to the altar was a sick-looking man. He was so thin that one could almost hear his bones rattling as he walked to the altar supported by a woman. As the sick-looking man approached the altar, Apostle Joseph burst into a diatribe against wicked people. He said the man's illness was man-made, that the culprit was a friend of the man's who was jealous of the man's success in business. Apostle Joseph appealed to God to destroy the powers of this diabolical man and the congregation shouted 'Amen' in unison.

The sickly-looking man and his supporter knelt down in front of the altar while Apostle Joseph prayed to God on his behalf.

When Ije's turn came, she walked up to the altar with her head bent. Apostle Joseph said that he could see God handing over to her a handsome baby boy. He said that all she had to do was to trust in God and to pray to him fervently every day. He blamed her apparent barrenness on a woman whom he would not name.

Ije knelt in front of the altar while Apostle Joseph beseeched God to break the powers of her enemies and to grant her her wish. The congregation shouted 'Amen' at the end of each sentence.

Three more new converts had their turns after Ije. There followed a general offering, and a final hymn brought the service to an end.

After the service each of the new converts had a private session with the apostle in the vestry. When Ije went to see him, he listed the things he needed from her in order to pray for her. These included twelve metres of yellow poplin, six packets of candles, and six big bottles of olive oil.

'In addition to this,' Apostle Joseph continued, 'you will fast for a week, eating nothing between six in the morning and six in the evening. Twice a week, at least, you'll come to the church for prayers.'

'Thank you very much,' Ije said. 'I'll do all that you've told me.'

Back home, Dozie listened to his wife's account of her first visit to the faith-healer's church.

'I don't like this idea of fasting, Ije,' he said. 'I don't want you to become undernourished.'

'I'll be all right,' Ije said. 'I can endure any inconvenience as long as it will help me get what I want. At least I am allowed to drink water between these hours. Some new converts have been forbidden from drinking even water between six in the morning and six in the night.'

Ugo Ushie did not think much of Apostle Joseph when she heard of Ije's first day in his church. It was on the tip of her tongue to ask what the apostle would do with the metres of poplin, the bottles of olive oil and the candles, but she controlled herself because such a question could undermine Ije's faith in the apostle. This demand by this 'man of God' only went to confirm the stories circulated about faith-healers who owned big shops where they sold the articles they demanded from their congregations. The offerings, of course, also went into their pockets.

Ije did not find her week of fasting unbearable. She took a cup of tea with plenty of milk and two slices of bread before six in the morning and this carried her conveniently to six o'clock in the evening. Dozie made matters easier for her by joining her in the fasting. He had reasoned that it would be tempting for Ije to cook his meals and to watch him eat his lunch. After two days of this experiment, Dozie commented that he liked it as it made him feel lighter and healthier. He added humorously, though, that initially the hunger pains had gnawed so hard into his stomach that he almost gave up the fasting.

During the following week Ije accompanied Dozie to Port Harcourt to collect his payment for designing a hotel for a firm there. They celebrated the occasion quietly and by themselves in their hotel. The one week they spent there was like a second honeymoon to Ije.

Back home at Enugu Dozie finished designing his dream house. He had consulted Ije throughout the designing and had included all the gadgets and amenities she would like to have in the house. He also designed a small bungalow which they would use as a guest house, and a small block of offices. His plot of land was a big one and would take all these conveniently; and the profit he made from his work in Port Harcourt was more than enough to pay for the buildings.

After a week of bargaining he signed a contract for the building of the houses with a well-known engineering firm based at Enugu. He took Ije into his confidence all the time and told her of all his moves, always seeking her opinion first before deciding finally what to do.

Dozie's fame as an architect rose by leaps and bounds. The contracts he won were more than he could handle alone comfortably, so he employed two architects to help him. These were two young men who had just finished their national youth service. He also engaged the services of an accountant to manage the accounts of his firm in order to give Ije more time for rest.

Ije's membership of Apostle Joseph's church was short-lived. For a month and a half she attended the services on Sundays, went regularly in the evenings for prayers, and made generous offerings to God through the apostle.

One evening, after prayers, Apostle Joseph said he would like to pray for Ije alone. When everybody had left, he prayed long and hard for her and after that he told her to come to the vestry with him. There he offered her a seat opposite his and began to talk about God working miracles through people like him.

He continued, 'God has revealed to me everything about you. You're a virtuous woman, a loving wife, who's as faithful to her husband as a dog is to its master. Am I right, Mrs Apia?'

'I don't know,' Ije said modestly. 'It is for other people

to say whether I am virtuous or not. I love my husband dearly, though.'

'I know I am right because God has told me everything,' Apostle Joseph went on. 'I wouldn't be telling you all this but for the respect and admiration I have for you. I would like to see you possess that one thing that remains to make your marriage perfect.'

He paused. Ije was surprised at the apostle's knowledge of her and her life.

'What I am going to suggest to you may sound atrocious to you, Mrs Apia, but I am making the suggestion out of love – not the kind of love we all talk about – I don't really know how to put it so that you'll understand me.'

'Go on, I understand,' Ije said.

Apostle Joseph shifted uncomfortably in his chair. Then he said, 'Do you know that sometimes God works his miracles through people – especially through people like us?'

Ije nodded.

The apostle continued. He was becoming a bit incoherent. 'Some men, for some reason, are unable to father children. Wise women who are married to such men tactfully find other men to give them what they so much desire. This is not adultery in the eyes of men. It is not adultery in the eyes of God. Think about this, Mrs Apia. I have gladly done it for some women. I can do it for you too.'

He stopped talking. The ordeal of what he wanted to say was over. Rivulets of sweat ran down his face. He brought out a handkerchief and mopped them up.

Ije was stunned. She remained silent only for a second.

'To hell with you and your church!' she cried and stalked out of the room, swearing never to set foot in Apostle Joseph's church again.

Chapter Seven

After several visits to Owerri, Dozie secured another contract for designing a small housing estate for a parvenu. In order to speed up the work, he opened a small office at Owerri and transferred a handful of his workers to the town.

Ije was pleased with Dozie's successes, but she detested the days and nights she had to spend alone because of Dozie's business trips. When he was away, she spent most of the mornings in the office although she had nothing in particular to do there. In the evenings she would either visit Ugo Ushie or stay at home to read magazines and novels.

One afternoon, when Ije came home from market, Teresa ran out to meet her.

'Mama is here again, madam,' Teresa said to her in a whisper.

Ije's heart missed a beat. The cold war that had existed between her and her mother-in-law had become so intensified that it had turned into open warfare.

'When did she arrive?' Ije asked Teresa.

'A few minutes after you'd left for market,' Teresa said, leading the way into the sitting-room.

'Where is she?' Ije asked in an undertone when she did not see Mama in the sitting-room.

'Sleeping,' Teresa whispered in reply. 'She's asleep in the guest room.'

Ije sat down in one of the armchairs. She pulled off her shoes and handed them over to Teresa.

'Put them away in the bedroom,' she instructed, 'and get me my slippers. Don't wake Mama up. I want to have a rest first before I meet her.'

Mama had brought so much trouble with her whenever she visited her son that Ije had come to dread her visits as one dreads a terminal disease.

Teresa took the shoes to the bedroom and in a minute she reappeared with the slippers.

Ije took the slippers from her. 'Tell James to bring my lunch,' she said. 'Warn him not to make any noise. I must eat and rest before Mama wakes up.'

'Yes, madam,' Teresa whispered and tiptoed into the kitchen, closing the door quietly behind her.

As Ije waited for her lunch, all the events of her last encounter with Mama became alive in her mind. She wished Mama had not come for she was not in the mood to go through another crisis. She wished she knew what had brought Mama to Enugu so that she would be able to forestall her.

'Madam, food is ready,' James said quietly, interrupting her thoughts.

She rose heavily from the chair and walked quietly

to the dining-table. She ate out of habit for she was not hungry. Her mother-in-law's visit had drained the appetite out of her. She took a sedative after her meal and in a short time she was sleeping dreamlessly in utter rest.

When she woke up an hour or two later, she decided to remain in bed for a while because she dreaded meeting Mama. In a short time she heard her voice, 'Teresa, is your madam still sleeping?' There was an undertone of hostility in her voice.

'Yes, Mama,' Teresa replied defiantly.

Mama continued, 'I don't blame her. Why can't she sleep for hours on end? Has she any work to do? Has she any children to look after?'

Ije shook her head sadly. She got out of bed, changed into a simple frock and went to the sitting-room to meet Mama.

'Welcome, Mama,' she said, hugging her. 'You were sleeping when I came back from market. How are the people at home?'

'No trouble,' said Mama. She did not return her daughter-in-law's warm smile. 'Where has my son gone?' she asked brusquely.

'He's gone to Owerri,' Ije said, sitting down. She turned to Teresa who had just walked in and asked her if Mama had been given her lunch. Teresa nodded.

'How long has Dozie been away?' Mama asked Ije.

'Two days.'

'When is he coming back home?'

'I don't know, Mama. He'll come home as soon as he finishes his business there.'

Mama turned to Teresa who was still standing near the door, waiting for an opportunity to speak to her mistress.

'Do they call you Tarasa, or what?' she snapped. 'Why are you standing there looking at me like that? Have you nothing better to do?'

The embarrassed Teresa was about to leave the room when Ije asked her kindly what she wanted. She whispered something into Ije's ear and left the room.

'Do you mean Dozie did not tell you when to expect him?' Mama asked.

'No, Mama.'

'I must see him before I go. And probably this is going to be my last visit to this house. Unless he takes his time and behaves like a man.'

'Mama, let me get you a bottle of cold stout,' Ije said, ignoring Mama's threat.

'If you like. Don't get me a cold one.'

Ije served Mama with a bottle of stout and some slices of cake. Mama sipped her drink and ate her cake without a word. Ije remained silent too for she did not know what to say without incurring Mama's anger. The cold war between them was a bitter one and she was at a loss what to do to make the cloud of distrust between her and her mother-in-law roll away and make them visible to each other. A grandchild would have succeeded in blowing the clouds away, Ije reasoned, but that was apparently beyond hoping for.

Ije heaved a sigh when the doorbell rang and James opened the door to let Ugo Ushie in.

'Welcome, Ugo,' Ije beamed. 'How are Ayo and the kids?'

'Fine,' Ugo was about to sit down when she noticed Mama. She went to her and embraced her lightly out of habit.

'Welcome to Enugu, Mama,' she said. 'I hope the people at home are well.'

'Yes.' Mama recognised Ugo Ushie, having seen her several times before in her son's house.

'Is Dozie back?' Ugo Ushie asked, sitting down.

'Not yet,' Ije replied.

'Absence makes the heart grow fonder, they say,' Ugo Ushie chuckled. 'I wish my husband would go away for a while, then I'd not have to step into the kitchen as long as he was away.'

'People rarely value what they have,' declared Ije. 'Dozie is travelling a lot these days. I wish he didn't.'

'Business expansion – and that means more money,' Ugo Ushie pointed out, smiling. 'Now don't let us forget Mama.'

She turned to Mama and asked her when she arrived.

'Today,' Mama replied.

'Did you have a comfortable journey?'

'Yes.' Mama's monosyllabic replies indicated that she was not in the mood for conversation. Ugo Ushie took the hint.

While Ije and Ugo sipped some orange squash and munched some cake, Mama pretended to be asleep, occasionally stealing a look at the two friends through the corner of her eyes. She had earlier declined another bottle of stout and a second helping of cake. A few minutes later she rose from her chair saying she was tired and was going into her room to rest.

'Good riddance!' Ugo Ushie exclaimed when Mama was out of hearing. 'At least we can talk freely now.' She knew all about the cold war between Mama and Ije and naturally her sympathy had always been with Ije.

Ije remarked in a whisper, 'Mama has come with a bombshell. I can see it from her face. I wonder what I have done wrong this time?'

'Don't let that worry you,' Ugo Ushie consoled her friend. 'You've been very good to Mama. You lavish money and gifts on her. You must know that very few women approve of their daughters-in-law.'

'But, Ugo, Mama is not grateful for all I do for her. That is not what she wants from me. She only wants grandchildren and I cannot give her any.'

'Is it your fault? Children come from God.'

'What have I done to make God deny me even one child?' Ije asked sadly.

'Nothing. You'll have your children, Ije. In God's own time.'

'I'm losing hope fast, Ugo. I'm not getting any younger.'

'Nonsense!' Ugo Ushie admonished.

Ije looked at her friend and wished she were like her. Nothing ever seemed to disturb the underlying calm of her life for she had a tranquillity, a perfect grip on herself that everybody admired. She would put her troubles away and forget them just as she would give away a frock she did not like and forget about it. She did not care about what people said about her, always dismissing such gossip by saying that her self-esteem did not depend on the opinion of other people.

'Do you know Uju is in hospital, Ije?' Ugo Ushie asked. Uju was their classmate at college.

'No. What's wrong with her?'

'I don't know. I was told she had had an operation. I've come to ask you if we can go and see her.'

'But Uju told me they were going to Aba on transfer?'

'Yes, they came here only about a fortnight ago. She and her husband have found jobs here.'

'Is that so? When do you want us to go and see her?'

'Now. I won't be in this weekend. We're going home to see my mother-in-law. She's not well.'

'Give me five minutes and I'll be ready,' Ije said.

She was ready in less than that time. Mama reappeared in the sitting-room just when they were about to leave. Ije told her where they were going. Mama asked her who Uju was and Ije told her.

A few minutes after Ije returned from the hospital, Beatrice called.

'You've not been attending Apostle Joseph's church for some time now, Ije,' Beatrice remarked as she sat down. 'Are you ill?'

Ije would have liked to lie but she was not accustomed to doing so and was afraid she would falter and betray herself. She therefore told Beatrice about the apostle's advances, leaving nothing out.

'Maybe you were luckier than I. I suppose he didn't suggest such a thing to you,' she concluded.

Beatrice remained silent for a while, then she said, 'I'll confide in you, Ije, for two reasons. You're so good that I'm sure you'll keep my secret. Moreover, if I confide in you, the guilt will be lifted off my chest and I'll feel better. This baby is Apostle Joseph's.'

Ije was shocked. 'You don't mean it, Beatrice!' she protested.

'I do, and I don't regret my action. My infidelity has saved my marriage, for my husband was on the verge of sending me away and taking a new wife. If my marriage breaks down now at least I'll have a child who will look after me in old age. A childless woman in our society does not realise the extent of her handicap until she grows old.'

As Ije remained silent, Beatrice continued, 'I have ceased to be emotional about my baby. In the circumstances, it is better for me to be practical. I hope, Ije, you will keep my secret? I'd do anything to keep my husband from knowing the truth.'

Ije promised to tell no-one, not even her own husband, about Beatrice's story. For hours afterwards she thought about this revelation. She tried to exculpate Beatrice, to understand the motives for her infidelity, and ended by saying to herself that she could never do such a thing. She had not lost all hope of having a baby for Dozie: a child that would have something from each of them and therefore bring them even closer.

Three days after Mama's arrival, Dozie returned from Owerri. Ije welcomed him with an affectionate smile and a warm embrace.

'D., you've been away so long,' she said.

'I'm very sorry I had to be. There was too much work for me there.'

'Hush, Mama is asleep. You'll wake her up,' Ije whispered to Dozie as they approached the guest-room.

'When did she arrive?'

'Three days ago.'

'Is she ill?'

'No. She says she's not ill.'

'Anything wrong at home?' There was a tinge of anxiety in his voice.

'No,' Ije reassured him. 'Mama says all is well at home.'

They were now in the bedroom. Dozie yawned loudly.

'Hungry or tired?' Ije asked.

'Both.'

Ije laughed. 'I'll soon cure you of both your illnesses.'

She did not consider it too late to cook her husband's favourite dish for him, neither did she bother to go and fetch James or Teresa who had retired for the night.

In less than an hour after arriving home, Dozie sat down to a delicious plate of jollof rice. He ate with unconcealed relish while Ije told him about the work in the office, and some little bits of gossip that were circulating in the town. She also briefed him about the progress made in building their house at Independence Layout.

Dozie said, 'I've got the job, Ije, and it's going to fetch me thousands of naira.' His face lit up.

'I'm very happy for you, D.,' Ije said, looking at her husband with misted, affectionate eyes. 'Oh, D.! You're doing wonderfully well.'

'I couldn't have done so well without you. I don't know what would have become of me if I hadn't married you …'

Dozie was speaking from the bottom of his heart. Ije had been the brains behind his successes. When he vacillated between resigning his job in the Ministry and striking out on his own it was Ije who came to his aid and urged him to take the plunge. The beginning was an uphill task — what with its disappointments and uncertainties. At that time jobs were not coming and very soon he had exhausted his savings in running about to secure contracts and in bribing his way.

Ije had kept her job and of her own free will had given him all her salary. Life was hard but she never complained. She made the housekeeping money go as far as possible and did not grumble because she could not afford to buy jewellery and new clothes. Through dint of hard work she had helped Dozie into becoming a rich and successful architect.

Soon Dozie's plate was empty. He belched satisfactorily and reclined in his chair. Ije cleared the table and soon afterwards they went to bed.

When Mama came into the sitting-room in the morning she was surprised to see her son sitting down to breakfast.

'Mama,' Dozie said, getting up to greet his mother, 'when I peeped into your room last night you were fast asleep. I did not want to disturb you.'

'When did you come home?' Mama asked.

'Last night. After you'd gone to bed. How are the people at home?'

'They are well,' Mama said, sitting down.

Dozie went back to his food and soon afterwards Ije came in with a plate of fried eggs.

'Good morning, Mama,' she said.

'Good morning.'

'What will you have for breakfast, Mama? There is tea and bread and there is jollof rice.'

Dozie cut in, 'Give her some of the jollof rice you cooked for me last night. I'm sure she'll enjoy it.'

'No, I don't want rice,' Mama protested. 'Give me tea and bread.'

Ije went back to the kitchen and in a short time she reappeared with Mama's breakfast.

Mama ate silently, dunking her bread into her tea and occasionally spooning the tea into her mouth.

'I hope the tea is not too hot for you, Mama,' Ije said concernedly.

'No,' Mama answered without lifting her eyes from her cup. 'Are you quite well, Mama?' Dozie asked.

'Yes.'

'Any trouble at home?'

'No.'

'What is the matter then? You don't look happy.'

'Have I any cause to be happy? I have come to discuss something with you. I want to go home this morning.'

'You can't go this morning, Mama. I have something important to do in the office so I can't stop to talk with you now. Let's leave it till this evening. Then you can go home tomorrow morning.'

He drained his cup and told Ije to hurry up as both of them were going to the office together.

Ije drained her cup and fetched her handbag from the bedroom. Then she told Mama that she had instructed James to give her whatever she asked for, and she and Dozie left.

'Now, Mama, what is it you want to talk to me about?' Dozie said later that evening.

Ije stood up to go in order to leave mother and son alone to talk, but Mama would not let her. According to her what she wanted to talk about concerned her too.

'Dozie, why have you kept on denying me a grand-child?' Mama began in a mournful voice.

'Mama, this is not of my own making.'

'Why can't you get a second wife?' Mama asked. 'What is wrong with marrying again when your wife cannot give you a child?'

'Mama, Ije is still young,' Dozie said, half-pleading,

half-asserting. 'I've planned for her to go overseas for treatment. She will leave in a short time.'

'Who says educated men don't take more than one wife?' Mama continued, ignoring Dozie's defence. 'I don't have to go far to give you examples. You know the doctor whose father's house is near ours. You know the "ingina" too. Are you more educated than they?' (Mama could not pronounce the word 'engineer' correctly.)

When Dozie said nothing, Mama continued, 'I know why you don't take another wife. Ije is the cause of everything. She has bewitched you! She has used medicine to make you not look at another woman. The medicine has even affected your attitude to me. You used to obey me, but now my words to you are as useless as pouring water on a stone.'

She turned on Ije. 'As from now your medicine will lose its potency — I'll see to that! I'll soon show you that some, medicines are stronger than others! And let me tell both of you; that I'll not leave you alone until you do what I want!'

Once again she began to disparage Ije. Once again Dozie failed to stop her. She went on and on until copious tears began to run down Ije's cheeks. She could bear it no longer. She rose from her seat and walked noiselessly into the bedroom.

For hours she lay awake because she could not sleep. Later she heard Dozie get into bed. It must have been past midnight — three hours after she had left him with his mother.

'Ije, I'm sorry about Mama,' Dozie said as he lay beside her. 'Don't let what she says bother you very much. No amount of threats or goading from her will make me do what I don't want to do.'

Ije remained silent. She was tired of crying and just lay there staring at the dark ceiling. She wished her own mother was alive to talk sense into her mother-in-law.

Dozie and Ije remained awake but silent; the silence between them was saying eloquently what they were afraid to say, while the currents of love and understanding which used to pass between them seemed to have come to a standstill. The night crawled, until one after the other, they were overcome with sleep – the balm of troubled minds.

Mama left the following morning. She refused to have any breakfast and only accepted her son's offer to let his driver take her home after half an hour of pleading. Ije packed some foodstuffs for her, but knowing full well Mama would reject them, she put them in the car secretly and instructed the driver to leave the foodstuffs with Mama when they got home.

For two days the events of Mama's visit damped the spirits of the Apias. They had a lot to say to each other about Mama's comments but somehow they dreaded saying it. It was becoming clear to Ije that Dozie was only postponing taking the initiative.

As more days came and went, they began to recover from the depression into which Mama's visit had plunged them, and in a week's time their relationship with each other had become normal once more.

Chapter Eight

Dozie made several trips to Owerri, either in connection with the work he had in hand there or to seek new contracts. Ije followed him to Owerri once and came home ill. The roads were full of pot-holes and the jolts she received in the car made her ache in every limb. Besides, she did not enjoy her stay in Owerri because Dozie was so busy meeting people and keeping appointments that he came back to the hotel where they were staying only after midnight each day.

Towards the end of February, Dozie and Ije travelled to their town for the launching ceremony of the town's half a million development fund. It was a red letter day for all those who attended the great occasion. For women, it was an opportunity to show off their gorgeous wrappers and expensive lace blouses. Ije, dressed in a simple 'Accra' long skirt and blouse, watched the 'fashion parade' and the women's display of vanity with amusement. She could not understand how some women who, she knew, could hardly afford three square meals a day, could afford the costly outfits with which they had adorned themselves.

Dozie stole the show that day. He donated a huge sum of money and his people were so overwhelmed by his generosity that they carried him shoulder-high and danced round the town square. Ije felt very proud of her husband and danced with the women as they made up impromptu songs in praise of Dozie Apia, 'the handsome man that carries his town on his shoulders.' Dozie's mother was very elated, too. Having shelved her disagreement with her son, she joined the women in dancing round the square and left no doubt in the minds of all present that she was the proud mother of the philanthropic Dozie Apia.

The launching ceremony ended just before dusk but Dozie could not leave the scene because so many people wanted to talk to him; to express their gratitude to him for his generous donation; and to request in the most subtle way his aid in some other projects which some 'age grades' had embarked upon.

Ije waited for Dozie under a big tree. She watched the large crowd disperse in groups, talking excitedly about the launching ceremony.

Two women came and stood near her, apparently waiting for someone. One of the women was fair and beautiful; the other made up in height what she lacked in beauty.

'That man, Dozie Apia, is very generous,' said the beautiful one. 'Imagine donating such a huge amount of money! He must be very rich.'

'Of course he must be very rich to part with such an

amount,' said the tall one. Then she added in a whisper, 'They say he has no children. His wife is barren.'

'True?'

'Yes,' affirmed the tall one.

'Ewo! Isn't it wicked to deny such a generous man children of his own? What is he going to do with his money if he has nobody to leave it to?'

'He'll certainly marry another wife unless he's a fool,' the tall one said.

'But he's a Christian, isn't he? And educated?'

'That doesn't mean he can't take a second wife if he wishes. The days are gone when a Christian or an educated man felt embarrassed to take a second wife.'

'I hear that his mother has fallen out with him many times because he won't marry again,' the beautiful one put in.

'I heard that too. But I bet you he'll marry again in his own time. He can't leave his money to distant relations alone.'

'Do you think it is true that his wife used "medicine" to prevent him from taking another wife?'

'Maybe. If it is true the "medicine" will certainly lose its potency one day and leave him free,' the tall one prophesied.

'Oh, here is Mgbeke. She's taken a long time coming.'

Mgbeke soon joined them and the three women walked home together. Ije, who had heard every word of the conversation, was relieved to see them go. Their words had pierced her heart like a dagger. None of them knew who she was or else they would not have discussed her in her presence. Or would they? It pained her to note from their conversation that she was seen as a fly in Dozie's ointment.

It was not until long after dusk that Dozie could extricate himself from the men who had stayed behind to talk to him. He found Ije waiting for him under the tree, apologised to her for keeping her waiting for so long, and took her home. They found Mama and her brother, Udo, having a tête-à-tête in the sitting-room.

Dozie expressed surprise that his maternal uncle had not gone back to his village about six kilometres away.

Udo, smiling, told him he was waiting to be taken home in his car.

'I want a ride in that beautiful car of yours,' Udo said again. 'But I'll wait for you to have your supper first.'

Mama and Udo talked in hushed tones while Dozie and Ije ate their supper silently. Ije had congratulated her husband on their way home and had told him the good things she heard people say about him.

After they had eaten, Udo told Dozie he wanted to have a chat with him. Ije politely left them and retired into the bedroom. She took a cold bath and lay on the bed. Later Dozie came in and told her he was going to take his uncle home. The two men had talked for hours.

'Is anything wrong, D.?' Ije asked her husband.

'Nothing in particular. I'll tell you what we've been talking about when I come back from driving my uncle home.'

Ije watched him change his clothes and shoes.

'I'll be back in no time,' he said.

'Let me go and say "goodbye" to Uncle Udo,' Ije said as she followed Dozie to the front of the house where Udo stood waiting.

'Goodnight,' Ije said to Udo.

'Goodnight, my wife,' Udo replied.

Ije watched Dozie and Udo get into the car. Mama got in too. She said she wanted to keep Dozie company on his way back.

Half an hour later, Dozie and Mama returned. Mother and son then stood outside and talked for about half an hour before Mama retired into her little hut to sleep.

'Are you sure nothing is wrong?' Ije asked Dozie as she walked into the bedroom.

'Nothing much,' said Dozie absent-mindedly.

Ije decided not to pry into the matter any further. She knew that Dozie would tell her in his own time what it was that his maternal uncle had talked to him about for hours. He did not hold back anything from her.

Back at Enugu, Dozie continued his work with vigour. He was a hard-working and intelligent man who knew his job well. His only flaw was his inability to take decisions easily and stick to them. Every change was a risk and he hated taking risks. In his moments of vacillation, his courageous wife had come to his rescue, giving him the courage to take the plunge, as when he left the government service to begin his own business. But in his work as an architect, he needed no help from anyone. He always knew what to do and did it. As he got on with his job, Ije took over the supervision of the building of their new house in Independence Layout. She saw to it that the contractor building the house did not slacken his pace.

Towards the end of March, Dozie had another feather in his cap: he was elected a member of the executive of an association of architects to which he belonged. It was a highly prestigious, nation-wide association and to be elected an officer one had to be recognised as competent and worthy of the honour.

The meeting in which Dozie was elected was held in Enugu, and to mark the end of the conference the Enugu branch of the association gave a cocktail party in honour of the delegates from other states.

The party had hardly started when somebody pinched Ije's ear from behind. She turned abruptly and was surprised to see Patience.

'Patience!' she beamed. 'What brings you here?'

'We've come back to Enugu for good,' Patience declared.

'When did you arrive?'

'Only two days ago.'

'How's your husband?'

'I left him down there talking with his friends.' Patience

pointed to a group of men talking together a few metres away. 'Where is Dozie?'

'I've lost him,' Ije laughed. 'He must be here somewhere.'

'I nearly called on you this afternoon,' Patience said.

'Why didn't you?'

'I had a visitor just about the time I wanted to leave for your house,' Patience explained.

The two women now moved about together and chatted with other women. They came across Mike, Patience's husband, who left his group and joined them.

'How's Dozie?' he asked Ije.

'He's somewhere around,' Ije said, looking around her. 'Oh, there he is,' she said, leading the way.

They soon came to Dozie and he too left his group to talk with Mike and Patience. They had exchanged only a few words when a woman joined them. She looked at Dozie and smiled at him in recognition.

'Hello,' she said, 'pleased to see you again.'

Dozie knitted his brow. He could not recognise the woman. She came to his rescue.

'We met twice in Miss Virginia Ujo's flat at Owerri.'

'I remember now,' said Dozie. He felt a little uneasy.

'I'm Mrs Ime,' the woman introduced herself. 'I don't know the members of your group.'

Dozie introduced Patience and Mike to her and lastly, Ije.

Mrs Ime looked bewildered. She opened her mouth to say something but stopped herself just in time. The observant Patience took in all this, but quite unlike her, she reserved her comments.

Dozie and Mike left the women to join their friends. Mrs Ime stuck to Ije and Patience as firmly as a tick sticks to a dog's ear. Apart from being priggish, she was also a name-dropper and when Patience could bear her no longer she tactfully got rid of her.

At last the party came to an end. On their way home Ije asked Dozie who Miss Ujo was.

'You've never told me about her,' Ije said without emotion.

Dozie explained, 'She's a friend of a friend.'

As Ije said nothing Dozie added, 'She's not important; that's why I did not tell you about her.'

Ije, who had always had implicit confidence in her husband, accepted the explanation and left it at that.

The next day was Saturday. A little after eight in the morning Ugo Ushie called at the Apias'. Ije was still in her dressing-gown.

'I'm sure you've forgotten we planned to go to Artisan market to buy a goat this morning,' Ugo Ushie said.

'Oh, dear! Indeed I did forget all about it. Let me get ready at once.'

'You know that the earlier we get there, the better bargain we'll get,' Ugo Ushie pointed out.

Ije rushed out of the sitting-room. In a few minutes she was back dressed.

'I'm ready,' she declared. 'D., I'm taking the driver,' she called to her husband. 'I hope you don't want to go out?'

'You can take him,' Dozie shouted from the bathroom. His muffled voice indicated that he had his tooth-brush in his mouth.

At Artisan market, Ugo Ushie and Ije bought a middle-sized goat. They paid a butcher to dress it and share it into two equal parts for them. After this they stopped at the main market to do some shopping. By one o'clock in the afternoon they were back home.

Chapter Nine

Two months glided by. Dozie grew rich by leaps and bounds. He secured one contract after another and as he was efficient in his work he carried these contracts out to the satisfaction of all concerned. In his generosity he took over single-handed the completion of his village church. All of a sudden he had become the darling of his people and his friends. He rarely refused anybody any favour as long as he could afford to grant it.

The contractor handling the building of his house in Independence Layout abandoned the job after extracting three times as much money as the work done. Dozie ignored his friend David's advice to sue this contractor and instead found another one to continue the work from where the unscrupulous contractor had left off.

Ije looked forward to June when she would go overseas for treatment. Dozie had promised to go with her so that they would combine a holiday with her treatment. She spent some of her time supplying the contractor with the building materials he needed.

One day, Dozie came back from Owerri looking sad

and agitated. This mood continued into the next day and to Ije's bewilderment, Dozie would not confide in her as before, although she pleaded with him to tell her what was troubling him.

'What's the matter, D.?' Ije asked her husband as his depression continued into the third day.

'Nothing,' Dozie replied.

'Yes, there is,' Ije said affectionately. 'There's something eating you. Why can't you tell me? Haven't we always been frank with each other?'

Dozie said helplessly, 'You can't do anything about it.'

'Never mind, tell me all the same,' Ije pleaded.

But Dozie would not tell her and she did not press him any more.

As his depression continued, Ije became more and more puzzled. She was used to Dozie's moodiness when he was on the verge of taking a major decision. But then he had always taken her into his confidence and the two of them had tackled the problem together, thereby making it easier.

'Why then,' Ije asked herself, 'won't Dozie confide in me this time?'

Not long afterwards, the cause of Dozie's depression manifested itself. On the morning of that day, Dozie left for a short visit to Onitsha, while Ije went to the office to help the accountant in bringing the accounts up to date. It was a tiring job and it was after two in the afternoon when she left the office, looking forward to a good rest at home.

When Teresa heard her drive into the compound, she ran out to meet her.

'Oh, not Mama again,' Ije said under her breath as she saw Teresa coming. Whenever she ran out to meet her before she came into the house, it was because she wanted to warn her in advance about something.

'Welcome, madam,' Teresa said.

Ije asked, 'Is Mama here, Teresa?'

'No, madam, not Mama, but one woman.' Teresa lowered her voice and continued, 'She came with three boxes and two travelling bags. It looks as if she has come to stay.'

'Who is she looking for?'

'Master.'

'Did she tell you who she is?'

'No, madam.'

'Where is she now?'

'In the sitting-room, madam.'

Ije was apprehensive as she entered her house. The visitor was relaxing in one of their deep armchairs. Her face was heavily made-up: bright red lips, thin arched eyebrows, rosy cheeks, and dull green eyelids – a smooth perfect mask. It was not easy to tell whether her fair complexion was natural or induced by bleaching-cream. She was dozing when Ije walked in.

'James!' Ije called in order to arouse the visitor.

The visitor rose with a start.

'Good afternoon,' Ije greeted her politely.

'Good afternoon,' she replied, looking Ije up and down.

Ije said, 'I understand you want to see Mr Apia. I'm sorry he's out of town and won't come back in time.' She sat down and began to pull off her shoes.

'By the way, I'm Mrs Apia,' Ije introduced herself. 'I don't think we've met before?'

The visitor said rudely, 'I'm Mrs Apia too. I'm carrying Mr Apia's baby and I've come to take my rightful place in his house.'

Ije was stunned. The room seemed to be spinning round, or was it her head? She wanted to scream, to call the visitor an impostor, a liar. But she braced herself and said as calmly as she could, 'There must be a mistake. Maybe you mean another Mr Apia.'

'Don't be stupid,' the visitor blurted out. 'I know whom I am talking about. I'm carrying Dozie Apia's baby. You are his childless wife, aren't you? I can't live outside with his baby while you, who have given him no child all these years, stay in and enjoy everything.'

'I'm sure there's a mistake,' Ije said, trying to be calm although she was inwardly greatly agitated. She felt the tears welling to her eyes, but she did not want to weep in front of this sneering woman. She blinked hard to stop the tears. The visitor said something else, but Ije was concentrating too much to hear her.

Ije went to the kitchen and gave instructions to James and Teresa. Making sure that the bedroom and guest-room were securely locked, she got into her car and drove away, her hands trembling on the steering-wheel. She made straight for Ugo Ushie's flat. It took her no longer than five minutes to get there but in that little time a multitude of emotions churned up her mind. She found Ugo Ushie eating her lunch.

'I'm ruined, Ugo,' she cried bitterly, and collapsing into a chair, she began to sob like a child.

Ugo Ushie left her food and went to her. 'What's the matter, Ije?' she asked, holding her friend's trembling shoulders.

Ije poured out, more in tears than in words, what had happened in her house a few minutes before.

She swore between sobs, 'I'll pack up and get out of that house if what that woman says is true. I can't ever forgive Dozie if he has done that to me.'

'You'll do no such thing,' Ugo Ushie cautioned. She had a wide knowledge of life and was reputed for keeping her head when all about her were losing theirs. 'How can you be sure the woman is not framing you, Ije? Even if her claims are true, you're not going to run away from your home, or are you? That will mean leaving all you have toiled for behind. And that will be doing exactly what this woman wants you to do, so that she can reap where she did not sow.'

At that moment Ugo Ushie's youngest child, U-U, ran into the room. On seeing Ije, he ran to her and then saw that she was crying. His face suddenly changed.

'Mummy, why is Auntie crying?' he asked concernedly.

'Run out and play, U-U,' Ugo Ushie ordered. The

bewildered boy looked at Ije again and slowly walked out of the room.

'Where is Dozie at present?' Ugo Ushie asked Ije.

'He's gone to Onitsha.'

'When will he come back?'

'Later today.'

'Ije, I advise you to go back to your house. Don't show this woman that you're worried by her presence. Treat her as a visitor, and if she becomes nasty, ignore her. Let her stay in the sitting-room until Dozie returns. And please, don't you ever take any decision when you're upset because you can't think clearly.'

She led her friend into the bathroom and made her wash her tearstained face with cold water. Then she took her into the bedroom and made her powder her face.

'Now, I don't want anybody, especially your visitor, to know that you've been crying. And get ready to put up a good fight for your rights just in case what the woman says is true. I'll come to see you tomorrow morning.' She paused for a while. 'Tomorrow is Saturday, isn't it?'

Ije nodded. She looked at her friend gratefully for she knew she could always count on her and on her practical and altruistic advice.

As she drove home she hoped to discover on arrival that the visitor had gone. But this was wishful thinking as she realised when she stepped into the sitting-room. There sat the woman, stiff with hostility, waiting, as unexcited and implacable as the sphinx. Ignoring her, Ije went about the house in her routine manner.

She was in the sitting-room with the visitor when Dozie arrived home late in the evening. She had planted herself there in order to be able to see Dozie's reaction on seeing the woman.

When Dozie walked in, Ije rose and went to him, embracing him ostentatiously.

'I didn't hear your car drive in, D.,' she said.

Dozie was about to say something when he saw the visitor. He was transfixed. The room seemed suddenly cleared of all the furniture.

'What are you doing here, Virginia?' he shouted at the woman.

'I've made up your mind for you,' Virginia said spacing out the words. Her equanimity was devastating. 'You can't continue to keep me out of your house when I'm carrying your baby, and when it is the first baby you're going to have.'

Ije waited for Dozie to deny Virginia's claim in vain. She stood there looking with unseeing eyes. Her mind seemed to have stopped working. Then she saw her husband through glazed eyes. He was standing like a post, helpless, confused, and full of remorse.

Gradually Ije came back to herself. She slowly walked into her bedroom and flung herself onto the bed. Dozie had violated his marriage vows and now she would be held up to ridicule and shame. Tears of anger, hurt, disappointment, regret and uncertainty flowed copiously down her cheeks. She did nothing to stop them. She must let them flow or they would choke the breath out of her.

She heard Dozie come into the bedroom and heard him leave. She heard James ask if he should serve Dozie his food. Dozie declined and said he was going out immediately.

Virginia remained in the sitting-room. Nobody had offered her food; nobody had offered her a room. Her luggage was still beside her.

After nine o'clock, Ije went to the kitchen and told Teresa and James that they could go to bed. She spoke as calmly as possible.

'I'm waiting to serve Master his food when he comes back,' James said.

'Never mind, I'll do that,' Ije said. 'I will eat with him when he comes back.' Her eyes were still red with crying despite her attempts to erase all traces of tears from them.

'Madam, what about the visitor?' James asked. 'Will I serve her some food?'

'We'll all eat when Master is back,' Ije explained. She was not going to do any such thing, but she had to prevent James from suspecting that something was amiss in the house.

James and Teresa locked up and went to their quarters. Ije returned to the bedroom and bolted the door. She lay on her back staring at the ceiling, her hands clasped beneath her head. She was trying to think.

Minutes later, she got out of bed and began to pack her things. She must leave the house at once in spite of Ugo Ushie's advice against such an action.

An hour and a half later, she heard Dozie drive in. For some time now he had been driving himself, having dismissed his personal driver for insubordination. He had refused to replace him with his office driver who, according to him, was incompetent.

Ije opened the front door for Dozie. She did not speak to him. They had not spoken to each other since Virginia's assertion and his failure to deny it. Ije carefully bolted the front door and went back to the bedroom. For hours now she had kept to that room like a mouse to its hole. Dozie stopped in the dining room to drink some water.

'I'm surprised at the way you've received me here,' Virginia reproached Dozie, as if she were talking to a child. 'You've been married for years without a child and now when there's one coming your way you treat its mother like a leper.'

Dozie sank into a chair and sat with his head in his hands. He cursed the day he had met Virginia at a weekend club in Owerri and, in a moment of unthinking weakness, fallen victim to her seductive approaches. He had joined a group of friends on a drinking spree at the club, and one of them had introduced him to Virginia. For once he had let himself go and had got drunk. Taking advantage of his drunken state, Virginia had enticed him away from the club and both of them had spent the night in her flat, about a kilometre away from the club house. It was a one-day affair for which, afterwards, he had felt some remorse but which he had since forgotten.

Months later, when he was again in Owerri, Virginia had sought him out to tell him that she was expecting his baby. At first he had been elated at the thought of being a father, but when he remembered his wife, Ije, and what effect the news would have on her, he had become scared.

Virginia had watched him closely as he battled with his conflicting emotions and had decided that she could exploit his naivety and desire for an heir, having learnt his situation from his male friends in whose company she moved. First, she had pleaded with Dozie to take her to his home and later threatened to move into his house and make him take responsibility for his action.

Back in Enugu, Dozie had been too scared to discuss his plight with Ije, and Virginia, true to her word, had barged into his house without any notice.

Now, the consequences of his one-day affair with Virginia lay heavily on him. He could not find an easy way out of the fix he had put himself in. He could not afford to offend or alienate either Ije or Virginia, for he needed them both. He loved Ije dearly and owed his success in life to her. She had been his helpmate and his stay and had made their home something without which his life would be unthinkable.

But he also needed Virginia, because she was carrying his baby, a part of him, and to throw her out of his house meant throwing away his baby, perhaps the only one he would ever have. He was not sure now that Ije would bear his children even after receiving treatment overseas.

He glanced at Virginia. She was looking tired and worn out.

'Have you had anything to eat?' he asked her.

Virginia stifled a yawn. 'Has anybody offered me any food in this house?' she asked. 'Maybe I won't even be offered a bed, either.'

'If you're sure you don't want any food, I'll show you your room.'

He took her to the guest-room and hauled her luggage single-handed to what was to be her bedroom. It was self-contained, with its own toilet and bath.

'I'll accept this room only for a while,' Virginia said with the air of one who always got her own way. She banged the door after Dozie had left the room.

After sitting alone in the porch for about an hour, Dozie went into the bedroom. He was shocked to see that Ije had packed her things. She was now sitting on the edge of the bed and her body was shaking with silent sobbing.

Dozie went and sat beside her. 'Please, Ije, do not leave me,' he pleaded. 'I'll be ruined without you. Please, Ije, I'll explain everything when your anger subsides.' He tried to put his arm round her but she shook it off violently and moved away from him. He made another attempt to plead with her not to leave him but met with a more violent rebuff.

Dozie left the house and in a few minutes Ije heard him drive away. When he came back it was past midnight. He decided to spend the night in the sitting-room.

Ije found it difficult to sleep. In her loneliness the blow of the whole incident became painful and unbearable. She began to plan about tomorrow. Where would she go? It must be a place where she could be swallowed up; where there would be no one who knew her. She decided to go to Lagos. She had enough money to stay in a cheap hotel until she got a job. She now realised why most women who were married to wealthy men insisted on making their own money or in putting away some of their husband's money and investing it in their own name.

She would wait for Dozie to leave for the office, and then she would go out and take a taxi. She had packed only her clothes, shoes and trinkets. She would take nothing more. She was going to start life anew. She must leave behind those presents given to her by Dozie as these would be a constant reminder of the very life she would do better to forget. Towards the early hours of the morning she fell into a tired sleep.

Very early in the morning the next day, Ayo and Ugo Ushie came to see the Apias. Dozie, afraid that Ije would leave him, had gone to them the night before and had appealed to them to come and plead with Ije not to leave him.

First, the Ushies reproached Dozie for going so far with Virginia without any hint to Ije. Ugo Ushie was sure that if

Dozie had told Ije that he wanted a second wife, Ije would not have stood in his way. Dozie did not try to defend his action. Rather he told them regretfully about his one-day affair with Virginia at Owerri, and ended by saying that although he did not love Virginia, he could not disown his child.

Next the Ushies appealed to Ije not to leave her husband. They reminded Dozie that Ije was still the mistress of the house and must remain so. On no account, Ugo Ushie warned, should Ije's position be undermined or usurped by Virginia. Dozie must see to that and should later find Virginia a flat in the town.

Ije, who had a violent headache and was weak with the tears and the traumatic experience of the night, remained silent throughout the Ushies' attempts at reconciliation. She was afraid that if she opened her mouth, she might begin to cry again.

But at last she decided to break her silence and unburden her battered mind. She said, in apparent calmness, that the whole thing was still like a nightmare to her. 'I still cannot get myself to believe that Dozie can be involved in such a silly scandal, Dozie whom I have always held so high above other men, Dozie whom I have always thought, and would have sworn any time, to be above such thoughtless infidelity. Dozie whom I… I…' She broke down and, sobbing inconsolably, left the room.

Ugo Ushie followed and had a separate session with Ije. She told her of a woman she knew who had found herself in a similar position, but had stayed on. Eventually, she had her own children which was what mattered to her most.

'And to have your own children is the most important thing, Ije,' Ugo Ushie said in conclusion. 'To have your own children who will look after you in your old age. A husband may forget his wife, but a woman's children are not likely to forget her. Don't you ever allow that woman to have everything while you lose it all.'

At last Ije decided to accept the situation but she knew that life would no longer be rosy; that she would have to put up a long fight for her rights. She shrank into herself and spoke no word more than necessary. For days on end she acted as if Dozie and Virginia did not exist. With a maudlin readiness to cry, she avoided their company as much as possible. Something was gone from her relationship with Dozie, and there began a period of coldness between them.

Chapter Ten

The news that Dozie Apia had taken a second wife spread like wildfire among his friends and acquaintances. It was discussed even by those who knew neither him nor his wife. Many versions of the incident erupted and each version ramified into different versions until no two people's accounts of the story tallied. All this gossip reached Ije's ears and made her miserable.

At first she shied away from her friends because she could not face their unuttered questions, nor their sympathy which was given in the hope of extracting the whole story or rather her own version of the story. She could not face the ever-increasing barrage of sneers and veiled insults from her so-called friends and from those she had gone out of her way to gratify.

Those who knew the Apias visited them in order to verify the story. Virginia, in her attempt to establish her position, made sure that each visitor saw her. She stayed in the sitting-room most of the time or came to the room on hearing a visitor come in.

Patience also came to see Ije. Virginia was sleeping

when she called, but Ije was in the living-room, turning the pages of a magazine.

'Ije, my dear, I am very sorry for what Dozie has done,' Patience said, sitting down. She was as trendy as ever.

'Well, that's life,' Ije said.

'Do you know how I heard the story?' Patience blared. She was the type that could nose out a scandal anywhere. She continued, 'Beatrice told me that when she telephoned you, a woman's voice answered and when she told the woman that she wanted to speak to Mrs Apia, the woman said she was Mrs Apia and banged down the telephone when Beatrice told her she was not the Mrs Apia she knew.'

'I've stopped listening to gossip,' Ije said.

'Where is she?" Patience whispered, looking mischievously around her.

'In her room,' Ije replied.

Patience said, 'Quite frankly, Ije, I don't know why you let her stay.'

'What do you expect me to do?' There was despair in her voice.

'If I were you,' Patience stated, 'either she would leave this house or I would leave.'

Ije made no comment.

Patience continued, 'You're too accommodating for my liking, Ije. No woman would dare do that to me and get away with it!'

'Let me get you something to drink,' Ije said, stopping the conversation. Patience was trying to probe a nasty deep wound which had scarcely begun to heal.

'No, my dear Ije,' Patience protested benignly, 'I'm not in the mood for drinks. I feel very unhappy about your plight. I think the whole thing is very unfair.'

Ije was about to say something when the door of the short passage leading to the guest-room creaked and Virginia entered. Without being told, Patience knew that this was the new wife, the woman who had succeeded where Ije had failed.

Ije hoped that Patience would not be as malicious as one of her so-called friends, who, in spite of the fact that she had heard all about Virginia and could guess very well that she was the one sitting opposite Ije, had asked Ije if Virginia was her sister. Ije had ignored the question and the woman had repeated it louder than before. Virginia had seized the opportunity to assert herself by introducing herself as Mrs Apia.

Patience looked Virginia over and tried to stare her out of countenance. Her eyes pierced through Virginia, penetrating her soul, trying to assess her; to see what type of woman she was.

Virginia greeted her and sat down. Patience mumbled a reply. It was obvious that she did not like Virginia. A few minutes later she stood up and told Ije she must be going.

'Thank you for calling,' Ije said, and followed her out.

'Listen, Ije,' Patience said immediately they were outside, 'You must be very careful with this woman. As soon as I saw her small deep-set eyes, I felt sorry for you. Only crafty and vicious people have such eyes. You know I can see through people easily. She looks a calculating woman; a woman who makes sure she gets what she wants; who knows on which side her bread is buttered. Bet you, very soon she'll be twisting Dozie round her little finger if you don't take care.'

Patience might be garrulous, but she was a good judge of character. Her assessment of Virginia was the same as Ugo Ushie's.

'I'll take care of myself,' Ije said to Patience and bade her goodbye.

With the arrival of Virginia, Dozie became a fugitive from his own house, taking refuge in his office and not in his club where his friends would ask him embarrassing questions. He felt uneasy in the presence of both Ije and Virginia. Ije had become more reticent than ever, while Virginia nagged him constantly for not treating her with the reverence which she deserved because of her condition. For weeks he slept on the settee in the sitting-room because he dreaded sharing a bed with either Ije or Virginia.

He scouted around and rented a flat, but when he told Virginia to move into it she would not hear of it.

'Aren't you ashamed to tell the mother of your baby to

live outside your home while a woman who's useless to you occupies it?' Virginia snapped.

'Ije is not useless,' Dozie retorted, and walked out. He did not raise the matter again, however, nor did he have the courage or the heart to ask Ije to move to the flat. He was now aware that from that point forward his life was going to be complicated; that the peace which had seemed so stable a part of his home was shattered.

James and Teresa were adversely affected by the new situation in the house. They moved about quietly and often talked in hushed tones about 'Master's action'. However, it was not difficult to see whose side they were on. Teresa did not hide her hatred for Virginia, neither did the new mistress forgo any opportunity of making Teresa know that she was only the maid after all.

Virginia, who knew what she wanted and how to get it, cornered Dozie by using the baby as a lure and made him furnish the guest-room where she slept as elaborately as he had furnished the bedroom he had shared with Ije. This was after her subtle attempts to dislodge Ije from the exquisite bedroom had failed.

Next she wanted Dozie to buy her a car like Ije's but since the model was no longer available at that time she had to settle for a less elegant and expensive car. Having noticed that money was no problem to Dozie, she demanded one thing after another, and Dozie had to oblige her if only to have some peace.

Ije had stopped taking any interest in the house being built for her husband in Independence Layout.

'What's the use of toiling so that another woman will be comfortable?' she confided in Ugo Ushie one afternoon. Ugo Ushie's house had become her bolt-hole, a place where she would go to have some solace whenever the situation in her own house became unbearable.

'I've told you many times, Ije, to hold on to what is yours,' Ugo Ushie reiterated. 'Besides, I don't like your attitude to Dozie these days. The more you alienate yourself from him the more you drive him into the welcoming arms of that scheming woman.'

'What do you want me to do?' Ije asked helplessly. 'Virginia has him under her thumb. He does whatever she tells him to do. Dozie desperately wants a child and Virginia is going to give it to him soon. What have I on him? Tell me?'

'Dozie does not love Virginia. That much I know. He wants the baby and is afraid of losing it. That's why he can't afford to offend her.'

'That's exactly the situation,' Ije stated. 'I don't want to fight a lost battle any more. I've lost Dozie to Virginia because I can't have his baby. In this situation, love is second-rate.'

'All the same, Ije, don't push Dozie completely to Virginia. June is not so far away. I'm sure that some treatment overseas will solve your problem. I'm sure too that Dozie will value your own baby more than Virginia's.'

A gloomy look came over Ije's face. She said, 'Now that Dozie has got what he's been longing for, do you think he will still want to pay for my treatment overseas?'

'Don't cross your bridges before you come to them, Ije,' Ugo Ushie advised. 'Old shoes are more comfortable than new ones, especially when the novelty of the new ones diminishes. You're losing weight fast, Ije. That means you have not been eating well.'

'I have no appetite,' Ije confessed. 'I am so unhappy.'

'I know you are. But remember, it's important to keep up your strength in a fight.'

Two hours later, Ije left Ugo Ushie's house after having an early supper with her. Ayo Ushie, who had been out visiting with the children, came home when Ije was about to drive away. The children were all happy to see her.

'Auntie, I want to come to your house,' U-U pleaded.

'All right, my dear,' Ije said, smiling at him, 'Mummy will bring you tomorrow.'

She drove away amidst their 'Bye-byes'.

When Ije arrived home, it was already dark. She went straight into the kitchen to see if James had finished cooking supper. Earlier that day, she had made up her mind to stop cooking the meals although Ugo Ushie had advised her not to do so.

She tasted the beans James had cooked and to her dismay, she found out he had put in too much salt. She shrugged her shoulders and told James to serve the food.

A few minutes later, Dozie, Ije and Virginia sat down to eat. Ije served herself from the big bowl and passed the bowl to Dozie who took a large helping because he liked beans. Virginia took only a spoonful. She told Dozie that she had instructed James to fry some eggs for her when Dozie wanted to know why she had taken such a small amount of food.

'This is not like your cooking, Ije,' Dozie said after tasting the beans. There's too much salt in it'.

'I didn't cook it. James did,' Ije said.

'Why?' Dozie asked.

'Because I've made up my mind to stop cooking the meals. Virginia can take over the housekeeping.'

'*I'm* not taking over anything!' Virginia snapped. 'In my condition I need a good rest every day.' She never failed to refer to her pregnancy whenever she was with Dozie and Ije.

'Nonsense!' Dozie thundered. 'Women in far more advanced stages of pregnancy than, you perform tasks that are more strenuous than cooking.'

'I don't care whether they do or not,' Virginia said defiantly. 'All I know is that *I'm* not going to do the cooking.'

'Ije has been doing it gladly until you came,' Dozie flared.

'I'm Virginia, not Ije. Besides, Ije is not pregnant. She doesn't know how tiring it is to be in such a state. And by the way, what is wrong in James doing the cooking? Most wives don't cook for their husbands if there are maids and house-boys to do it. You could even afford to employ a real chef.' She said the last word with an air of importance.

Ije ate her food silently. There and then she decided to eat alone from that day onwards. It was only at table that the three of them were likely to be together, thus giving Virginia the opportunity to gloat over her misfortune.

From that day onwards, too, it fell to James to go to market and buy food items and to cook, with Teresa assisting him. A week later, he packed his things and left, because he could not bear any longer the maltreatment meted out to him by Virginia. Ije was sorry to see him go. He was a quiet, undemonstrative and trustworthy lad, who would be difficult to replace.

When James left, Teresa took over his chores grudgingly. Ije, feeling very sorry for her because of the amount of work she had to do alone, resolved to help her by doing her washing herself. This did not lessen Teresa's laundry, however, because Virginia, who had taken to going out endlessly, apparently to exhibit her numerous newly acquired outfits, brought out a pile of clothes for washing every other day.

One afternoon, when Dozie came home for lunch, Teresa was only halfway through the cooking. Dozie flared up, and after a tirade, threatened Teresa with expulsion if he came home next time to find lunch not ready. As if Dozie's harsh words were not enough for Teresa, Virginia came out of her room and berated her vituperatively.

Teresa went back to the kitchen and continued with the cooking amidst tears. Ije, who had listened to Dozie and Virginia from her bedroom with disgust, went to the kitchen and helped Teresa with the cooking. In a short time lunch was ready. Ije smiled to herself as she watched Dozie consume his first helping of garri. He had not eaten so ravenously since she stopped cooking the meals.

Virginia noticed Dozie's good appetite, and knowing the cause decided to discredit her rival, Ije, who she knew had cooked the food.

'I don't like the taste of this soup,' she said with a grimace.

Dozie ignored the remark and took another large helping of garri and soup.

'Ije, won't you reconsider taking charge of the meals once again?' he asked.

'I will not,' Ije said emphatically.

'I don't see what you like in this soup,' Virginia complained.

Dozie again ignored the remark. He knew Virginia was eager to pick a quarrel with him but as he was not in the mood for that, he decided not to give her the opportunity she was looking for. No one spoke again until the meal was over. Dozie left for his office immediately and Virginia went into her room to sleep till late in the evening as was her custom. She would stay out all morning, come in just before lunch, and then sleep after lunch till five in the evening, when she would dress in the height of fashion and take a prominent seat in the sitting-room.

Ije sat alone on the balcony. In a short time Ugo Ushie would come to see her and both of them would visit a friend who had just had a baby. Presently, Teresa came to the balcony, and stood a little apart.

'Anything wrong, Teresa?' Ije asked.

Teresa sniffed. 'Yes, madam,' she said.

'What is it?'

'Madam, it is for your sake that I have been in this house up till now,' Teresa said with tears in her voice. 'The new madam is treating me badly. Even Master has joined her in scolding me all the time, even when I have done nothing bad. And look at what she's doing to you, too. You, who have treated me like your little sister. Every time you're away, the new madam tells Master lies about you. I'm tired of staying in this house! I'm tired of...' She burst into tears.

Ije got up and went to her. 'Stop crying, Teresa,' she consoled her. 'Life is like that. Don't worry about me. I'll be all right. I know you work far too hard in this house. I'll look for someone to help you, but meanwhile I'll do my best to help you.' She patted her kindly on the shoulder.

Teresa's crying subsided to a silent sobbing. 'I'm very

grateful to you for staying because of me,' Ije continued. 'I'll not forget that. Now stop crying and go to your room. One day things will be all right again.'

She hoped it was true.

Chapter Eleven

Mama arrived one rainy afternoon. She had heard that her son, Dozie, had taken a second wife, but she would not believe the story until she had seen things for herself.

Teresa, looking out of the kitchen window, saw her getting out of a taxi. Before she went out to help Mama bring in her luggage, she alerted Ije.

'Where is my new "Missisi"?' Mama asked immediately she entered the house.

Teresa ignored the question.

'Are you deaf?' Mama shouted at her. 'Didn't you hear my question?'

'Sorry, Mama, I didn't hear you, my mind was far away,' Teresa apologised.

'At your age!' Mama hissed. 'Where is my new "Missisi"?'

'She's not in, Mama.'

'Where has she gone?' Mama asked, sitting down.

'I don't know, Mama. She goes out every morning and comes back just before lunch.'

'Does she go to work?'

'I don't think so.'

'I hope she doesn't. What does she need a job for? And in her condition, too. When those as flat-bellied as men stay at home all day!' She peeped into her bag and began to look for something.

'Get me some water to drink,' Mama said to Teresa. 'Not that type that pulls out my teeth. By the way, where is the other "Missisi"?'

'She's sleeping,' Teresa said and left the room.

'White woman! What else can she do but sleep?'

Teresa came in with a glass of water. Mama took it from her and gulped it down. Just as Teresa was leaving the room, Ije came in. She had been listening to Mama from her bedroom.

'Welcome, Mama,' she said light-heartedly in spite of the weight on her mind.

'O – O', Mama said.

Ije embraced her and sat down. Mama had shown no warmth in her embrace but Ije was used to her coldness by now.

'How are people at home, Mama?'

'They are well.'

'How are our uncles?'

'They are well,' Mama replied. 'Is Dozie still at work?'

'Yes, Ma.'

Ije waited for Mama to ask her about Virginia but she did not.

'Let me get you something to drink, Mama,' Ije offered.

Mama accepted. Ije went to the kitchen to help Teresa prepare some food for Mama. For a moment she wondered where Mama would sleep since Virginia had taken over the guest-room where Mama used to sleep during her visits.

'Well, that's Dozie's headache, not mine,' she almost said aloud.

Virginia came back a few minutes after Mama had finished her meal.

'Are you my new wife?' Mama asked her.

'Are you Dozie's mother?' Virginia asked in return.

'Yes,' Mama replied. 'Now are you my new "Missisi"?'

'Yes, Ma,' Virginia answered in her softest tone. Ije just sat there watching the drama.

Mama rose from her chair and embraced Virginia warmly. 'Welcome, my wife,' she said. 'God bless you, my new wife. So it is true that you're pregnant already?'

Mama began to fondle Virginia's belly. 'Oh my child,' she cried with joy. 'I'm sure it is going to be a boy – a carbon copy of my son, Dozie. So these my eyes will see a grandchild, eh?'

She knelt down and raised her hands in silent supplication to God. She got up and began to sing Virginia's praises. She talked about the unborn child, and made indirect remarks about Ije's barrenness. Virginia, pleased with the praises showered on her by her mother-in-law, subtly encouraged her to go on.

Ije listened to all this without a word. Never in her life had she felt so friendless and forsaken as in the company of these women. She felt hot tears rush to her eyes and blinked hard to suppress them. She picked up a newspaper and buried her face in it. She did not want Mama or Virginia to see the tears that refused to be suppressed as she remembered the cold welcome she had received from Mama when she and Dozie arrived from England. She had been particularly hurt because she had expected Mama to show gratitude to her for helping Dozie financially.

Virginia sat down importantly. With each foot she prised the shoe off the other. Then she called Teresa to take the shoes to her room and fetch her slippers for her.

When Teresa handed the slippers to Virginia, she called her a stupid girl and told her it was not the pair she had asked her to bring.

'The blue soft slippers, fool!' Virginia snapped at her.

After two more trips to Virginia's room, Teresa succeeded in fetching the pair Virginia wanted.

Dozie came home for lunch later than usual. As he walked into the house, Mama showered him with praises.

'Now you have acted like a man, my son! At last you

have done what has been expected of you! If death comes this moment I'll gladly accept it, I will gladly go to my forefathers now that I have got a grandson.' She spoke as if the child had already been born.

Dozie felt embarrassed by Mama's words, but remained silent.

Mama continued, 'I wonder who had talked you into taking a second wife at last. Maybe you realised you'd been waiting in vain, or maybe her medicine has lost its potency.' She cast a side glance at Ije who was sitting beside her.

Virginia was enjoying her mother-in-law's taunts and insinuations but Dozie was not.

'That's enough, Mama,' he said. He could not keep his anger out of his voice or his face.

'What is enough, my son?' asked Mama. 'Anyway, since I've got what I want, let me leave it at that.' She turned to Virginia and said, 'Thank you, my "Missisi". You have saved my face. My enemies will no longer mock me; they will no longer act as if they have everything and I have nothing. Please, my new wife, take good care of yourself, and of my grandson.'

Dozie rose and left the room. After so many weeks, he still felt on edge whenever he found himself in the presence of his two wives. Now his mother had added to the uneasiness. He went to his study where he could have some peace.

When Dozie came home in the evening he brought

with him a small folding bed and a mattress to fit it. Since Virginia had taken the only extra bed in the house, he had to provide another one for Mama.

'I want to put a bed here for Mama,' Dozie said to Virginia who was lying down on her bed in the guest-room.

Virginia sat up. 'You'll do no such thing!' she said to Dozie. 'You'll have to find another place for her.'

'Where else can she sleep?' Dozie asked.

'That's your problem, not mine. All I know is that she's not sleeping here.'

'Aren't you being unfair to Mama after she has received you so well? What do you think she'll say if she hears you have denied her a place to sleep?'

'She's entitled to her opinion just as I am entitled to mine,' Virginia said with an air of finality.

Dozie looked hard at her for a minute. She could be charming when she wanted to be. She could also be extremely recalcitrant when it suited her. Dozie did not want to quarrel with her with Mama in the house. For one thing, Mama would certainly take her side. For another, and this would be humiliating to him, Mama would know from the turn of the quarrel that he had no authority over his new wife.

He walked like a hurt dog. He went to his study, a clutter of a place, and tried to make room for the bed. He needed somebody to help him shift the bookshelves and drawing equipment, but would not go to anybody for help; not to Virginia because of her condition, and not to Ije because he feared a rebuff.

Ije helped Teresa to prepare supper because Mama was in the house. While she was in the kitchen, Virginia chatted with Mama in the sitting-room. Dozie, as usual, had taken refuge in his office.

'Turn down the gas after the stew has simmered for some time,' Ije instructed Teresa.

'Yes, madam.'

'And don't add anything more to the stew – no water, no salt. Just turn it occasionally with a spoon.'

'Yes, madam. Will I cook some greens?'

'Oh, yes. Do not over-cook them.'

'I will not, madam.'

Ije left the kitchen, shutting the door quietly behind her. In the sitting-room she tripped over Virginia's slipper carelessly left in the middle of the room. She nursed her wound for a while. 'Can't you be a little tidier, Virginia?' she asked. 'I've warned you before about leaving your slippers in my way.'

'Have you no eyes in your head?' Virginia retorted, feeling no compunction for causing her co-wife injury. She littered things and would not be corrected.

Ije's simmering annoyance turned into boiling indignation. She opened her mouth to say something, but thought better of it. Instead she hissed and walked away. Extreme anger always left her dumb.

'This house does not belong to you alone,' Virginia shouted after her. Contempt edged her words. 'It's mine too, and I'm going to behave as I like in it. Who are you to direct me in this house?' She talked on and on until Mama, who had gone outside to look around, came in and asked her what the matter was.

'It's Ije,' Virginia shouted. 'She won't let me feel free in this house. She thinks the house belongs to her alone. Imagine that!'

'Don't mind her,' Mama said, sitting down. 'You have more claim to this house than she does. Don't let her upset you.' And for minutes she lectured Virginia on how to demand and get her rights in the house.

As usual, Mama's visit was a short one. She always preferred her little hut in the village to any other abode, no matter how luxurious, and would not listen to any plea to stay for more than a couple of days at Enugu.

Ije, feeling humiliated and unfairly treated, did not pack any foodstuffs for Mama to take home. She heaved a sigh of relief as the driver drove away with Mama at the end of her three-day visit.

In the evening of that day, Ugo Ushie called to see Ije.

'Where is she?' Ugo Ushie asked, pointing to the guest-room with her pouted lips.

Ije, of course, knew that Ugo was referring to Virginia.

'She's out. She's always out these days. I wonder where she goes.'

Ugo Ushie sat down comfortably. She felt freer with Ije when Virginia was not around.

'Where's Dozie?' she asked.

Ije replied, 'In the office, probably. Anyway he's not here.'

'He's overworking himself these days,' Ugo Ushie observed. 'He's grown older within a short time and bags are beginning to form under his eyes. I don't like his condition, Ije.'

'He brought it upon himself.'

'You're right, Ije, but if anything happens to him now you'll be very much the loser. Can't you persuade him to see a doctor? He looks ill. I'm sure he doesn't sleep well.'

Ije said meditatively, 'I don't think anything is wrong with him physically. But to tell you frankly, Ugo, that bond between us is no longer there. I can't talk to him intimately any more. He's like a stranger to me. I can't believe that we were so close before.'

'I can understand you, Ije. You still feel very hurt. Time will heal the wounds, I assure you.'

'I don't think so,' Ije said. She paused for a while and continued, 'Ugo, I'm thinking of taking a job. I can't stand the atmosphere of this house any more. If I get a job, I'll feel better. At least I'll be away from the house for some hours. I'll meet people, and I'll have some hours of peace. I must look elsewhere for solace.'

'Why not wait until you've been to England for

treatment? If you get a job now, you won't be granted your annual leave until after some months. And it won't be proper to ask for sick leave after working for only a couple of weeks.'

Ije pondered for a while. 'You are right, Ugo,' she said. 'But I want to be away from this house as long as I can each day. I can't come to your house in the mornings because you go to work. You're the only one I can still talk to freely since Virginia came.'

'I understand your problem, Ije,' Ugo Ushie consoled her friend.

Ije became silent, staring unseeing before her. Then she said, 'As a matter of fact, I'm thinking of moving out of this house.'

'You'll do no such thing!' Ugo Ushie protested vehemently. At that moment Virginia came in with two women. All three were tittering like weaver birds. As Virginia was not on speaking terms with Ije and her friends, a sudden silence descended on the sitting-room immediately she entered with her friends.

Ugo Ushie rose to go, and Ije followed her outside, leaving the sitting-room to Virginia and her tittering friends.

'I was going to tell you something about Virginia when she butted in with her fashion-crazy friends,' Ugo Ushie said.

'Patience has told me all about her,' Ije said. Patience was the type that could nose out a scandal anywhere.

'Oh, did she? Trust her to get information about people!'

'She told me Virginia was married before to a top government official in Owerri. She had one son by this man but they separated after a few years of marriage.'

'Patience's story corresponds with the one I heard,' Ugo Ushie declared. 'Do you think Dozie knows all about her?'

'I don't think so,' Ije said meditatively. 'I heard Virginia tell one of her friends that she would soon bring her child to Enugu, but her friend advised against it. Ugo, don't you see Virginia has the edge over me in so many ways?' Her eyes became clouded.

'Do you think Dozie will allow her to bring a child that is not his to his house?' Ugo Ushie thought aloud.

For a moment Ije did not answer. Then she said slowly, 'I don't know. I've ceased being able to read his mind. That's all the more reason I should get out of his house.'

'I repeat, Ije, you'll do no such thing.'

A car turned into the driveway. It was Dozie coming back from the office. Ugo Ushie waited for him to park the car in the garage. Then she went over to greet him. They talked for a minute and she rejoined her friend.

'I'll be going,' she said. 'I'd forgotten that Ayo wants the car at six. He'll be waiting for me now.'

'Thank you for all your help,' Ije said gratefully. 'I don't know how I could have survived without you.'

'Forget it,' Ugo Ushie said and got into the car. She let in the clutch and drove away.

Ije watched the car leave the driveway and join the street. Then she turned and walked slowly back into the house.

Chapter Twelve

'I'll be leaving for Owerri tomorrow and I'll be away for about a week,' Dozie said to Ije and Virginia one night. They were in the sitting-room watching television.

'I'll go with you,' Virginia said. 'I want to go and see my people.'

'I'm not taking you with me,' Dozie said emphatically. 'It's not safe for you to travel in your condition. The roads are very bad.'

'Nonsense! As if I'm an egg!' Virginia retorted.

Ije remained silent. It pained her to hear Dozie refer to Virginia's 'condition' like that in her presence. Neither he nor Virginia had experienced the agony of a childless woman listening to other people discuss what she was pining for but could not get, otherwise they might have spared her the heartbreak.

For some time now, Dozie had virtually transferred his belongings to Virginia's room. For all her faults, Virginia knew how to win people, and gradually she had won Dozie over. Sometimes it seemed as if she had got him in her pocket.

Ije found it disheartening to note that although Virginia often inveighed against Dozie and treated him with disrespect, a thing she never did herself, he had become closer to Virginia and further away from her.

Dozie left for Owerri the next day. He did not take Virginia with him, although she had grumbled all night and sulked from the time she woke up in the morning till Dozie drove out of the compound.

Two days later Ije suddenly became ill. It started with a rigor. She took two tablets of an analgesic and covered herself with two blankets. In spite of all these, she shivered like an electric fish pulled out of water. She made several attempts to call Teresa's attention but failed. She remained in bed until Teresa came into the room to tell her that lunch was ready.

'Madam, madam!' Teresa shouted with fright when she saw Ije shivering under the blankets. She could hear her teeth chattering.

'Go and call Mrs Ushie,' Ije managed to say between chattering teeth.

Teresa dashed out in a flash, and in less than an hour she was back with Mr and Mrs Ushie. Ugo Ushie had brought some malarial drugs with her. From Teresa's incoherent report of her mistress's illness, she had suspected that Ije was having an attack of malaria.

'Get her some water,' Ugo Ushie said to Teresa. The agitated girl flew out of the room. Ugo Ushie sat down on the bed and touched her friend's forehead. It was burning hot.

'She has a terrible fever,' she exclaimed. Ayo Ushie, who had been standing near the bed watching the shivering figure, bent down to verify his wife's verdict.

'You're right, Ugo,' he said. 'Don't you think we should take her to a doctor?'

'Not yet. Don't you remember how I cured myself when I had a similar illness last year?'

Ije began to murmur something.

'What is it?' Ugo Ushie asked, bending down to hear her friend better. Ije became silent again. 'I hope she doesn't become delirious,' Ugo Ushie said, looking up at her husband.

Teresa came in with a glass of water in a saucer. Ugo Ushie took it from her and cajoled her sick friend into taking four anti-malarial tablets.

'I hope she's not allergic to what you have given her,' Ayo Ushie said to his wife.

'That's no problem,' Ugo Ushie said importantly. 'If she is I'll give her something to stop the itching.'

Teresa stood and watched her mistress with watery eyes. Ugo Ushie, noticing Teresa's agitation, assured her that her mistress would soon be well again and coaxed her into returning to her domestic chores.

Some minutes later, Ije began to sweat. She threw off the blankets and opened her eyes. Ugo Ushie bent down and asked her how she felt.

'Better,' Ije answered faintly.

Next Ugo Ushie went to the kitchen and helped Teresa

prepare an appetising meal for Ije. While she was with Teresa, Ayo kept an eye on Ije.

'We'll come back in the evening and take you to a doctor for a thorough check-up,' Ayo Ushie said after Ije had eaten the meal served her.

'And stay around, Teresa, in case she wants you,' Ugo Ushie instructed. Teresa was standing at the foot of the bed still looking crestfallen.

'And you don't need to be so sad,' put in Ayo Ushie. 'You can see Madam is getting better already.'

A few minutes later, Ije fell into a peaceful slumber. The Ushies tiptoed out of the room. They found Virginia in the sitting-room. She had put up her legs on a low stool and had a plate of chicken on her lap. She was holding the two ends of the drumstick with her hands and digging her teeth into the flesh.

Ugo Ushie eyed her angrily. 'Ije is not well, do you know?' she asked Virginia.

'Yes,' Virginia replied, unconcernedly, intent on her chewing. 'I'm not surprised she's fallen ill. She's been tearing herself to pieces trying to fight me. She's wasting her energy because I won't budge. She's the one to suffer.' She dug her teeth once again into the flesh and began to chew the meat as if nothing ever worried her.

Ugo Ushie looked hard at her. She was about to say something to Virginia when her husband stopped her by nudging her.

'Let's go, Ugo,' he said, leading her away.

Teresa ran to meet them outside, expressing her gratitude to them as best she could. Ugo Ushie reassured her again that her mistress would be all right and told her they would be back in the evening.

When the Ushies came in the evening to take Ije to the doctor, she complained of a splitting headache.

'Migraine, perhaps,' Ugo Ushie said to her husband.

'I wonder where and when you studied medicine, Ugo,' Ayo Ushie chaffed.

'Experience is the best teacher,' Ugo retorted. She turned to Ije and asked her which doctor she wanted to be taken to.

'I want to go to my doctor at Uwani,' Ije said faintly. She was now sitting on the edge of the bed. Her eyes were swollen.

'All right,' Ugo Ushie said. 'We'll wait for you in the sitting-room while you get ready, or do you need any help?'

'No, I don't,' Ije said.

While the Ushies were waiting in the sitting-room, Virginia appeared. She was gorgeously dressed.

'We're taking Ije to see a doctor,' Ugo Ushie informed her.

'It does not concern me,' Virginia said and in a few minutes the Ushies heard her drive out of the premises.

'I wonder why you like talking to that woman,' Ayo Ushie remarked.

'Just to see her reaction; to know what goes on in that big head of hers. She's grown more beautiful since she came here.'

'Good food and no money problems,' Ayo Ushie declared. They were talking in hushed tones so that Ije would not hear them and get more upset.

Before they left for Uwani with Ije, Ugo Ushie locked Ije's bedroom and handed the key over to Teresa, instructing her not to give it to anyone except Mr Apia if he came home in Ije's absence. Ije had once complained that one day she found Virginia rummaging through her possessions in her bedroom and when confronted, Virginia had asked if she had not the right to do what she pleased in her husband's bedroom. It was for this reason that Ugo Ushie had decided to lock the bedroom and give the key to Teresa.

'Don't bother to cook any food for Madam, Teresa,' Ugo Ushie said. 'She'll eat at my house after she has seen the doctor.'

Teresa nodded.

'Now go and get some supper for yourself,' Ugo Ushie advised.

It was not easy getting to Uwani from G.R.A. Ayo Ushie was driving and Ije and Ugo were sitting in the back of the car. The traffic flowed easily until they came to the State Library. From then on the cars crawled like giant tortoises. On one side of the road were numerous market-men and women trudging home after the day's business, the women talking with their hands and mouths as they walked.

'We should have taken the Coal Camp route,' Ugo Ushie said when their car had stood still in the traffic for minutes.

'That route is even worse than this,' Ayo Ushie said. Somewhere ahead tyres screeched. Someone had jammed on his brakes to avoid a collision.

'I hope that's not an accident,' Ayo Ushie said. 'If it is we're not getting to Uwani today. We'll be kept here while the drivers of the vehicles argue for ages who is right and who is wrong.'

Ije had not said more than two sentences since they left her house. She was too weak to talk and was sometimes lost in thought.

They reached the doctor's clinic just before seven in the evening. There were a lot of patients in the waiting-room. The doctor's clerk knew Ije very well, and as she was one of those special patients who did not have to wait their turn, he told her to go in immediately the patient inside the consulting-room came out.

The Ushies went in with Ije and after exchanging greetings with the doctor left him with his patient. Some minutes later, Ije came out and told Ugo Ushie that the doctor wanted to see her to give her a message for someone.

'I won't be long,' Ugo Ushie said. 'Better get into the car and stay there. I'll join you in a minute.'

She walked into the consulting-room, closing the door gently behind her.

'Your friend's blood pressure is high,' the doctor said to Ugo Ushie.

'I'm not surprised, doctor.'

'Neither am I,' the doctor said. 'I can imagine how much stress she's undergoing. She told me her husband is away on tour – that's why I want to talk to you instead. I have given her some drugs to bring her blood pressure down, but you have to help her as much as you can. Help her to take her mind off her problems.'

'I'll do my best, doctor,' Ugo Ushie promised.

'See that she gets a good rest. If her blood pressure does not go down in a matter of days, I'll get her admitted to the teaching hospital.'

'I hope it won't get as bad as that, doctor.'

'I pray it doesn't. She's pretty bad.'

'Thank you very much doctor. I'll do my best for her,' Ugo Ushie said as she left the consulting-room.

But Ije's condition did not improve, and two days later, she was admitted to the teaching hospital in town. Her doctor had referred her to a friend of his who was working in the hospital. She was given a special room at the end of the female ward. As Dozie was still away, the Ushies had taken her to the hospital and had stayed with her until she fell asleep.

Ije stayed in the hospital for a week before she was discharged. For her the days in the hospital were a period of meditation; a period of taking stock of the events of the past couple of months. While in the hospital she took a decision which was to change the pattern of her life but not even Ugo Ushie, her best friend, was to know about it lest she talked her out of it.

Four days after Ije was discharged from hospital, Dozie came home. He was genuinely sorry to learn of Ije's illness. Ije did not tell him much but the Ushies did when he went to express his gratitude to them.

'Please, Dozie,' Ugo Ushie pleaded, 'see that Virginia does not upset Ije. If you lose Ije – well, let me not think about it.'

'I'll – I'll…' Dozie stammered. He could not continue. His face showed the agony in his heart.

Ugo Ushie looked at him out of the corner of her eye and shook her head sadly. He had lost weight and bags were beginning to form under his eyes. She could even spot some strands of grey hair in his head and beard – a sign of stress, she thought. The worst misfortune that could befall a man in Nigeria was to be childless, and only a Nigerian in a million would not take a second wife if the first one failed to bear him a child – and not just a child but a son. But, Ugo Ushie reasoned, Dozie should have taken Ije into his confidence before he got himself involved with Virginia. And to do what he had done after planning to send Ije overseas for treatment was not easy for Ugo Ushie to explain away.

When Ije had recovered fully from her illness, she found herself a job on the advice of her doctor. She did not want to go back to the insurance company where she had worked before because she could not stand the unuttered questions and insinuations by her former colleagues, nor their dubious sympathy and malicious gossip.

Her new job meant that she saw less of Virginia, and also helped to take her mind off her worries. Besides, it made her less dependent on Dozie financially although he had not failed to meet her monetary demands which were at this time rare and far between.

Virginia continued to keep Dozie under her thumb, using the baby to blackmail him. Sadly, Ije watched her husband become more and more like potter's clay in Virginia's hands, and Virginia, like a dexterous potter, moulded the pliable Dozie to the shape she wanted him.

Chapter Thirteen

June was only a couple of weeks away but Ije did not look forward to it any more since her continued estrangement from Dozie. One afternoon an incident occurred which was to sever the thin thread that joined them together.

When Dozie came home for lunch, Virginia told him in Ije's presence that she had seen Ije sprinkling some poison into their food. Ije was shocked to hear such an accusation. She laid down the magazine she was reading and asked Virginia to repeat what she had just said. She did so.

'Why did you do such a thing, Ije?' Dozie asked.

Ije's amazement was transmuted into anger and bitter disappointment when she heard Dozie's question.

'Dozie,' she said, using his full name for the first time for many years, 'does that mean you're condemning me without hearing from me? Has it come to the stage where you doubt my integrity? Do you now see me as a diabolical woman? Dozie,' she concluded, looking at him steadily, 'You are no longer the man I married.'

She said no more. She went to the dining-room, turned the soup vigorously with a spoon, put some soup in her plate, and scooped it into her mouth. She turned to Dozie and Virginia.

'This is to show you that I am innocent of your accusation,' she said and stalked out of the room. In the twinkling of an eye she was out of the house in search of a flat of her own.

She drove through all the streets in New Haven, but did not succeed in getting one. All the unoccupied flats she saw had already been rented. She drove to Uwani and luckily she found a good flat in the less congested part of the quarter. The landlord said he did not give his flats to single women and when Ije informed him that she was married, he asked her to bring her husband to see him.

'But my husband has gone overseas for further studies,' Ije lied.

'Where do you live at present?' the landlord asked.

'We lived at Onitsha before, but I have just been transferred to Enugu,' Ije lied again. She almost gave herself away because of her faltering.

The landlord looked at her steadily. His small eyes seemed to pierce her soul, her whole being, in order to get at the truth. A few free women had fooled him before so he had to be wary.

'Well,' he said, 'you'll have to find a guarantor, somebody I know who can stand surety for you.'

Ije was becoming frustrated. This was the only empty flat she had found which had not already been promised to someone so she could not afford to lose it.

'I'm new in the town,' Ije lied for the third time. 'I don't know anyone who knows you. Can't you trust me? You can eject me if you find me wanting.'

'How many children have you?' the landlord asked.

'Oh dear, what will this man not ask me?' Ije said to herself. Then she told the landlord that she had no children.

'You're newly married, I suppose?'

'No,' Ije said, 'I've been married for some years now.'

The landlord's face softened. 'Never mind. You're still young. You'll have your children in God's own time.' He agreed to rent her the flat but demanded six months' rent in advance.

'I usually ask for at least two years' rent in advance, but since your husband is away I'll take less from you.'

Ije expressed her profound gratitude, and left.

The next day, after work, she drove to Uwani to pay the rent. On her way home she stopped at a furniture company and paid for some pieces of furniture. By the evening of the same day she had bought everything she needed for the flat. She had procured only the essentials because she was not sure she was going to stay long in Enugu.

* * *

'I'm leaving this house, Teresa,' Ije said two days later. She had called the girl into her bedroom. Dozie had gone back to his office after lunch and Virginia was in her room. Adaku, Dozie's distant cousin, who had come to live with them a few weeks before, was also out.

'Then I'm leaving with you, madam,' Teresa said. It was then that she noticed the packed suitcases in the corner of the room.

'But I want you to stay and cook Master's meals,' Ije pleaded. She was surprised that a soft spot for Dozie still remained in her battered heart.

Teresa said, 'Madam, she will kill me if I stay in this house without you. If you don't want me to go with you I'll go home to my people.'

Teresa was an orphan and home to her meant going to her aunt in the village, a woman she detested. She had told Ije all about herself a few weeks after her arrival in the house.

'I'll take you with me, Teresa,' Ije said tenderly. 'Now go and pack your things as quickly as possible. I must leave here before Master comes back.'

When Teresa was ready, she helped Ije pack her luggage into the boot of the car. Virginia came out of her room and watched them without a word. Ije drove away without looking back after the suitcases had been hauled into the car.

She stopped at Ugo Ushie's. U-U was playing outside.

As Ije did not want to go into the flat she asked U-U to fetch his mother.

Presently Ugo Ushie came down. 'Aren't you coming in?' she asked.

'No,' Ije shook her head. 'I just came to tell you I'm leaving.'

'Leaving where?'

'Dozie's house. I've had enough.'

Ugo Ushie was dumbfounded. 'Where are you going?' she inquired.

Ije told her. 'Promise me you won't tell Dozie, or anyone else for that matter, where I'm going?'

'I don't like this, Ije. Why didn't you let us discuss this move first?'

'I didn't want you to stop me. I'll tell you the whole story later. You won't tell anyone where I'm going, will you?'

'I'll do as you wish,' Ugo Ushie said, and watched her friend drive away. 'I hope she's not going to do anything drastic,' she said aloud as she walked back to the flat.

Dozie came home after seven that evening. He went into Virginia's room to change and found her sitting on the bed, putting her hair in curlers.

'Go and tell Teresa to serve supper,' he said to Virginia.

'Teresa is not in.'

'Where has she gone?' Dozie said, taking off his shirt.

'I don't know.'

'What do you mean?' There was an edge to his voice. He had had a bad day at the office.

'I don't know,' Virginia said again, picking up a curler from her lap.

'Teresa is not usually out at this time,' Dozie declared and walked out of the room.

In the sitting-room he pressed the bell and sat down heavily in an armchair. Adaku, his cousin, appeared.

'Good evening, sir,' she greeted him.

'Good evening. Where is Teresa?'

'I don't know. I didn't see her when I came home from my typing lesson. Food is almost ready.'

'Where is madam?' Dozie asked.

Adaku hesitated. Then she asked, 'Which madam, sir?'

'The big one,' Dozie said, a little embarrassed.

'I don't know, sir. She wasn't in when I came home. Maybe she has gone to see Mrs Ushie.'

'Go and get my supper,' Dozie said.

He walked into the bedroom which he had shared with Ije to ask her for an important document he had given her. For some weeks he had not entered that room. Virginia had forbidden him to do so or she would leave him. And that to him would mean losing the baby.

A cursory look around the bedroom showed him that Ije's personal belongings were gone. He was puzzled. Had the room been burgled, or had Ije removed her possessions from the room? He was gripped with apprehension. He went to Virginia's room and asked her where Ije had gone.

'Since when have I become Ije's keeper?' Virginia answered back.

'When did she leave the house?'

'Did you tell me to keep a watch on her?'

Dozie looked hard at Virginia. He had had a bad time in the office and the effect was still on him.

'If you must know,' Virginia said nonchalantly, 'Ije left with her belongings. She took Teresa with her. Good riddance!'

'You don't mean it!' Dozie shouted. He was greatly agitated.

'Since when did you become so attached to her again?' Virginia taunted.

Dozie stalked out of the room. He felt as if a part of him had been violently cut off. Ije had been a part of him and now she was gone.

He sent Adaku to go and see whether Teresa was in her room. In a short while she returned to say that there was nothing in her room but her bed. Adaku, too, was feeling bad now that she had come to realise the true situation. She was a well-behaved girl who had become attached to Ije after only a few weeks of living with her.

In less than five minutes, Dozie had changed into fresh clothes and was on his way to the Ushies'. He found them in the porch in front of their flat. Ayo was picking his teeth which indicated that he had just had his supper.

The Ushies noticed Dozie's agitation.

'Do you know where Ije has gone?' Dozie asked. There was a tremor in his voice.

Ugo Ushie was silent for a moment. Then she said, 'I know where she has gone, but I gave her my word I would not tell you.'

'Please, Ugo,' Dozie pleaded.

'I will not break my promise to Ije. She will not forgive me if I do.'

'Please, Ayo,' Dozie turned to Mr Ushie, 'appeal to your wife to tell me where Ije has gone.'

'I'm sorry, Dozie, I can't. Nobody, not even me, can prevail on Ugo to do what is against her conscience.'

Dozie was crestfallen. He stared with unseeing eyes from his seat beside Ayo's.

'Even if I tell you where Ije is,' Ugo Ushie said to Dozie, 'I'm not sure she'll agree to see you. Give her a few days and her anger may subside.'

'Ugo is right,' Ayo said. 'If you go to Ije now she may refuse to see you. Meanwhile, Ugo will try and talk to her.'

When Dozie left the Ushies he thought of going to David, but changed his mind. David and some of his other friends had stopped coming to his house as often as they did before the arrival of Virginia. After enjoying

Ije's hospitality, these men had found it embarrassing to sit with Dozie and Virginia in the Apias' sitting-room while Ije kept to her room. David had tried to persuade Dozie to make Virginia move to a flat and when his advice was not heeded he had become a bit cool to Dozie.

For two days Dozie moved about like a shadow. He thought of going to see Ije in her office but he decided against it when he imagined how humiliated he would feel if Ije were to turn him out of her office in the presence of other employees.

Virginia was surprised at the effect Ije's departure was having on Dozie, for she had not expected him to feel Ije's absence at all. She did not like this turn of events and so decided to pursue her own plans before her grip on Dozie slackened. For some time now she had been trying to get a large sum of money from Dozie in spite of the considerable amounts he had given her earlier. She was one of those women Patience had talked about: women who did not believe in joint ownership in marriage but in having their own separate bank accounts or investments.

Three nights after Ije's departure from the house Virginia turned to blackmail to get what she wanted from Dozie. He refused to give her the money and she threatened to walk out on him.

'That baby you're carrying is mine,' Dozie exploded, 'so wherever you go I'll come and claim it.'

'How can you claim the baby is yours?' Virginia jeered.

'Wait till it comes to that,' Dozie fumed.

'I had better tell you the truth now,' Virginia shouted shamelessly. 'The baby is not yours. I chose you as its father because you're the richest of the lot – and because you wanted a child so badly. Do you call yourself a man? Look here, if you don't give me that money I'll tell the world about you. Wait till all your friends know you for what you are!' She rattled on and on.

Adaku was standing by the dining-room door listening to the hot exchange of words. Virginia continued to vituperate, while Dozie, dumbfounded, watched her. When she used a derogatory vernacular word to accuse him of sterility he could bear it no longer. He was so furious he would have beaten Virginia black and blue if Adaku had not thrown herself between them. Virginia escaped into her room and bolted the door.

Dozie sat in the sitting-room for the best part of the night. Virginia's words kept on ringing in his ears. Did she mean all that she had said? He knew that some women, when they were angry, would say a lot of nonsense, or accuse others falsely. All the same, he could not tell about Virginia. Did she mean it, when she said the baby was not his? Was she trying to blackmail him or was she speaking the truth? He wished he know the answers to these and many other questions that drummed in his ears.

Very early the next morning, he left the house and did not come back until it was dark. He removed all his possessions from Virginia's room and transferred them to his former bedroom. There he carefully packed a suitcase and then went to bed.

By six o'clock the following morning he was dressed ready to go out. He locked his bedroom and study. Then he gave Adaku some money.

'I'll be away for a week or two,' he said to her. 'Look after the house and if you're in any difficulty go to the Ushies and ask for their help.'

He brought out his car from the garage, put his suitcase in the boot and drove off. He stopped at the Ushies. Only Ugo was in.

'I'm leaving for London,' Dozie said to her.

'So sudden?' Ugo Ushie said. 'Anything wrong?'

Dozie ignored her question. 'How is Ije?'

'Fine. I saw her yesterday.'

'Does she still not want to see me?'

'No. Give her time.'

'I've driven all round Enugu in the evenings hoping to see her car parked somewhere. I've had no luck.' He was silent for a moment, then he said, 'Look after my house, please, Ugo. I've removed all valuables. I expect to be away for a week or so. And ask Ayo to keep an eye on my house in Independence Layout.'

'What about Adaku?' Ugo Ushie inquired.

'She'll stay. I've told her to come to you if she's in difficulty.'

'I'll do my best. Safe journey,' Ugo Ushie said. She watched Dozie drive away and she felt sorry for him.

Chapter Fourteen

It was from Adaku that Ugo Ushie learnt of the quarrel between Virginia and Dozie before the latter left for London. From Adaku's incoherent account of the altercation, Ugo Ushie concluded that money must have been the bone of contention.

Ugo Ushie received this piece of information the day after Dozie's departure and in the evening of the same day she went to Ije and narrated the whole incident to her.

'I've ceased being interested in what happens in that house,' Ije said. But the expression on her face belied the indifference in her words.

'You shouldn't say that, Ije,' Ugo Ushie reprimanded.

'Well, it's true. It was not easy for me to break with Dozie but I had to do it to save my life. It is impossible for me to describe the agony in my heart when I stayed in that house and watched Virginia manipulate him like a potter manipulates clay. It would have been different if I did not love Dozie with all my heart. At least when I'm here I don't see what happens in that house. To know is to be unhappy and ignorance, they say, is bliss.'

'Dozie has gone to England,' Ugo Ushie said. 'He didn't tell me what he was going there for, though.'

Ije made no comment as if to underline her earlier statement that she had ceased to be interested in Dozie and his affairs.

Ugo Ushie said, 'Now, Ije, where do you go from here?'

'I haven't made up my mind yet. Just now I want to be alone so that I can think without anyone disturbing me. One thing I am sure of, I am not going to marry again. A barren woman is useless as a wife, at least in our country.'

Ije tried to hide the pain in her heart but her friend was shrewd enough to recognise it. She knew the amount of confidence Ije had had in Dozie before Virginia came between them, and it pained her now to note that Ije had lost hope of all men.

Ije continued, 'I had always believed Dozie was above board. I don't think I can vouch for any man again, except of course your husband, Ugo. I don't think Ayo will ever be unfaithful to you. He. rarely goes out alone and he lets you know about all his movements.'

Although Ugo Ushie agreed with Ije's opinion of Ayo, her husband, she did not say so lest she fanned the animosity in Ije's heart. She changed the subject of their conversation, and thirty minutes later, she was gone.

Apart from Ugo Ushie, no one else had come to see Ije. She always parked her car inside the yard where nobody who knew her would see it. She still would not allow Ugo Ushie to tell Dozie where to find her.

'If you do that without my consent,' she had threatened Ugo, 'I'll have a clean break with you, too.' After this statement, Ugo Ushie was wise enough not to raise the subject again. She could hear the note of desperation in her friend's voice as she uttered the threat.

It was also from Adaku that Ugo Ushie had learnt of Dozie's mother's visit. On hearing that Ije had packed up and left the house, the woman had exulted openly. 'At last my son is becoming sensible,' she was reported to have said. Two days later she could not stand Virginia any more or perhaps it was Virginia who could not stand her. Mama hurriedly packed her things and left for the village unceremoniously. Ugo Ushie could imagine what was in Dozie's mother's mind as she travelled back home.

Exactly two weeks after Dozie had left for London, he came home. After unpacking, he drove straight to the Ushies'. It was evening and as usual Ayo had gone to the Sports Club to play tennis. Ugo was in the sitting-room with U-U who was tearfully demanding something from her. Dozie gave him some money and told him to go to the kiosk nearby and buy whatever he liked.

'When did you get back?' Ugo Ushie asked Dozie.

'Only a few minutes ago.'

'How was your trip?'

'Rewarding and revealing. Ugo, I must see Ije. You must help me see her at once.'

'She will not like to see you,' Ugo said quietly.

'You *must* help me, Ugo. You must persuade her to see

me. No one else can. I must see her. And for your information, I'm sending Virginia out of my house.'

Ugo was incredulous. 'What has she done?'

'Many things. She either leaves my house quietly or I throw her out.'

'What about your baby?'

'It is not my baby for all I know.'

'I don't understand you,' Ugo Ushie said, her big eyes bulging with amazement.

'You will understand me later. But first, help me by coaxing your friend, Ije, to let me come and see her.'

During the evening of the next day, Ugo Ushie went to see Ije, but she was away. Teresa told her Ije had gone to market. As her husband wanted the car in the next hour, she could not wait for her friend.

'Tell madam I'll call again about this time tomorrow,' she said to Teresa and left.

Back home she found Adaku waiting for her. She must have been crying because her eyes were red and swollen. In between sniffs she narrated her story. Dozie and Virginia had had their biggest quarrel a while before and Dozie had told Virginia to leave his house at once. Virginia would not budge so Dozie had thrown her belongings out of the house. Neighbours and passers-by had watched the scene, some shaking their heads sadly while others saw it as a big joke.

The story baffled Ugo Ushie. She calmed Adaku down and sent her back.

'I can't understand Dozie,' Ugo Ushie said to her husband over supper, after she had told him Adaku's story. 'I can't imagine him taking such drastic action. Dozie, who used to shy away from decision-making!'

Ayo drank some water and said, 'A man never stops growing. Besides, when you drive a man to the wall and there is no other way open for him to escape, he turns round and fights for his life even if he's been a coward all along.'

'I think you're right, Ayo.'

The next evening Ugo Ushie went to see Ije. She was at home. She rarely went out in the evenings.

Ugo Ushie came to the point at once. 'Dozie is back and he wants to see you, Ije,' she said.

Ije shook her head vehemently. 'I don't want to see him,' she said.

'Of course you must see him, Ije. I will be failing in my duty as your friend if I accept your refusal to see him. I'm bringing him here whether you like it or not. If you're out we'll sit here and wait for you until you come home. I'm sure you have no other place to sleep so you must come back here.'

Ije remained silent and Ugo Ushie continued. 'You see, Ije, Dozie is repentant and wants to come back to you. I'm sure he has had a revelation but he won't discuss it with me or any other person but you. You must give him another chance. And remember, a good wife must not allow her husband to humiliate himself before her.'

She paused for a while and said, 'It might interest you to know, Ije, that Virginia has gone.'

'What happened?' Ije could not hide her curiosity.

Ugo Ushie told her all she knew. Ije listened attentively but reserved her comments. Teresa served them with the *moi-moi* she had just finished cooking. They ate in silence. Ije had become reticent, as she always did when she was upset or confused.

When Ugo Ushie finished her plate of *moi-moi*, she rose to go.

'I'm bringing Dozie to see you,' she repeated.

'My people have a proverb which says that a wound may heal but the scar remains,' Ije said, 'and this scar always serves as a reminder to you so that you won't allow yourself to be wounded again.'

'Yes, that is true, Ije. The scar remains but we scarcely notice it. And even when we do it does not hurt any more and we scarcely remember how we got it. Time heals all wounds, they say.'

'Not the kind of wound I have,' Ije said sadly.

'*All* wounds, I say,' insisted Ugo Ushie.

Ije saw her friend downstairs and bade her goodnight. For the best part of that night she debated within her mind whether to see Dozie or not. There was no question of staying away from her flat because she knew Ugo Ushie would carry out her threat. She decided, therefore, to remain at home in the evenings but she made up her mind not to talk to Dozie no matter what happened.

* * *

It was past five o'clock in the evening. There was a knock at Ije's door. She told Teresa to open it. 'If it is Master,' she said, 'tell him I'm out.'

'Yes, madam,' Teresa said. She went to the door and cautiously opened it a little. Seeing only Ugo Ushie, she opened the door wide. As Ugo Ushie entered, Dozie followed on her heels. Teresa stood transfixed. There was nothing she could do now.

Ije was in the bedroom, so Ugo Ushie took Dozie there. When Ije saw them she shouted at Ugo Ushie to take Dozie away.

'I don't want to see him,' she cried, and then began to sob. She threw herself on the bed, her face buried in her pillow.

'You'll have to see him, Ije,' Ugo Ushie said and, shutting the door, tactfully left them alone. She had come in her own car and there was no need for her to wait for Dozie to take her home.

Dozie sat on the edge of the bed and waited for Ije to let off steam. When her wailing turned to whimpering, he moved nearer to her and gently turned her over. She was now weak with crying but she no longer refused his overtures.

'I'm extremely sorry for all I've done to you, Ije,' Dozie said. His voice was loaded with grief, remorse, and regret. 'I don't want to defend my actions because I can't. I've wronged you in every way. All I ask of you is to forgive me. I've made a grievous mistake in life but I promise you I'll never do such a thing again. I've learnt my lesson and I've learnt it the hard way.'

He continued to plead with Ije to forgive him, while she listened without a word. A keen observer, however, would notice the softening of her heart from her eyes.

Dozie now told her why he had gone to England and the outcome of his visit.

'I'm sorry that you've subjected yourself to all kinds of treatment, unpleasant ones and dangerous ones, when I have all along been the cause of our childlessness.'

Ije gazed at him in amazement.

He told her in the minutest detail of the examinations and tests he had undergone in a clinic in London. The tests had revealed that he had a minor blockage, but the doctor had assured him that the fault could be corrected by a simple operation.

'I've come, Ije,' he said, 'first to ask for your forgiveness, and second, to take you to London so that you'll be with me while I undergo the operation.'

After a short pause, he continued, 'I've sent Virginia away. She was an impostor because the baby she's carrying is not mine. I'll continue to curse the day I met her till the end of my life.'

He coughed and continued, 'If you'll forgive me, Ije, I'll arrange for you to have your inoculations as soon as possible, and we'll be able to leave for London in a week's time.'

He looked tenderly at Ije. 'Please, Ije, say something,' he entreated. 'Please say something to me. Don't just sit there looking at me.'

Ije began to cry again, but this time it was a cry without pain. Dozie recognised it and a look of relief passed over his face like a soothing hand and wiped away his tension. Virginia's episode was a blessing in disguise, he thought. Without it he would not have thought of submitting himself for a test.

Ije had the same thought, but neither of them expressed it. Once again their minds had begun to work on the same lines. Once again the current of love and understanding which used to pass between them before Virginia arrived to disrupt it, began to flow again in the familiar way.

About the Author

IFEOMA OKOYE was born in Anambra State, Nigeria. She graduated from the University of Nigeria in 1977 and went on to study at Aston University in England where she obtained a postgraduate degree in English. She taught as a Senior lecturer of English at Nnamdi Azikiwe University until 2000.

As well as being a prominent children's and short stories writer, her adult fiction has received numerous awards such as the prestigious Nigerian National Council of Art and Culture award in 1983 with her novel *Behind the Clouds*. She also won the 1985 Ife National Book Fair award and was the African Regional winner for the Commonwealth Short Story Competition in 1999.

She currently lives in Enugu, Nigeria. You can follow Okoye on Twitter at @ifeokoye.

Printed and bound by CPI Group (UK) Ltd, Croydon, CR0 4YY

20/03/2026

02075571-0001